Stratagem

Also by Jacques Vallee

In English:

Anatomy of a Phenomenon (Regnery, Ace, Ballantine)
Challenge to Science (Regnery, Ace, Ballantine)
Passport to Magonia (Regnery, Contemporary)
The Invisible College (E.P.Dutton)
Messengers of Deception (And/or, Bantam)
The Edge of Reality (with Dr.J.A.Hynek, Contemporary)
Dimensions (Contemporary, Ballantine)
Confrontations (Ballantine)
Revelations (Ballantine)
The Network Revolution (And/or, Penguin, Google)
Electronic Meetings (co-author, Addison-Wesley)
Computer Message Systems (McGraw-Hill)
A Cosmic Samizdat (Ballantine)
Forbidden Science (North Atlantic, Marlowe)
The Four Elements of Financial Alchemy (TenSpeed)
FastWalker (Frog Ltd.)
The Heart of the Internet (Hampton Roads, Google)

In French:

Le Sub-Espace, novel (Hachette – Jules Verne Prize)
Le Satellite Sombre, novel (Denoël, Présence du Futur)
Alintel, novel (Le Mercure de France)
La Mémoire de Markov, novel (Le Mercure de France)
Les Enjeux du Millénaire, essay (Hachette Littératures)
Au Coeur d'Internet (Balland, Google)
Stratagème (L'Archipel)

Jacques Vallee

Stratagem

A novel

Published by Documatica Research, LLC.

The author can be contacted at:
1550 California Street, suite 6L
San Francisco, CA. 94109

Website: www.jacquesvallee.com

Princeps edition
Copyright © 2007 by Documatica Research, LLC.

ISBN: 978-0-6151-5642-2
Registered with the WGA (Writers Guild of America, West)
No. 1077845

Printed in the United States of America.

July 2007

Stratagem:

A cleverly contrived trick or scheme
for gaining an end.

Webster's New Ideal Dictionary

Part One

NANOTRONICS

1

When the crisis began, I was in charge of business development at Nanotronics, a semiconductor company based in San Bruno, a San Francisco suburb. We had relocated there a few months before, and were now in a modern office building that towered above the runways of the international airport and the Coyote Point marina.

Apart from the small harbor with its pleasure boats, nothing distinguished San Bruno among the warehouse monotony and suburban sprawl that threatened to engulf the northern half of Silicon Valley. In summer evenings, the temperature gradient between the Pacific Ocean and the California interior created a thick layer of fog that rushed through a gap in the coastal range to obliterate all; in winter we were battered by storms that swept across San Francisco Bay. But the climate was never extreme, so that in all seasons the region continued to ignite the dreams of tourists and immigrants alike.

I have a sharp recollection of that particular morning. I reached the office about 8 A.M., filled with a sense of foreboding. For over a month, Mark Harris had been assuring me that final production of the B-7 system was imminent, but we were not seeing any results and our investors were getting nervous. Attorneys for the Goldenstar Fund were calling me almost daily to ask about the project's status. In tense voices, they alluded to an impending requirement to inspect our laboratories from one end to the other. They threatened to trigger a full technical and financial audit.

"It takes nerves of steel to do this job," I thought as I watched the floor numbers light up in sequence on the elevator screen, alternating with bright-colored promotional spots tempting me with car-rental rebates, ecological holidays in Borneo and a new DVD by Madonna. "At 48, I ought to find more sedate work, far from the stresses of high-tech and Silicon Valley."

When the Internet bubble burst, people had lost fortunes in a few short weeks. The premature claims of electronic commerce, promising to make our lives easier and launch a new economy, had ruined thousands of families, vaporized the pensions of workers and destroyed the job market in an area where full employment had long been the rule. Over 200,000 engineers and skilled technicians had left California with heavy hearts and empty wallets.

I knew something about that. The last barb Susan had thrown at me when we separated was still echoing in my mind. We had lived in Palo Alto. Perpetual spring put touches of splendor over the magnolias along the avenues; it spread blue foxglove and mounds of rosebushes in every garden. Once the movers' trucks had turned the corner and disappeared, she had climbed into her Toyota for the trip back to her folks' house in Colorado and told me:

"Life isn't measured in nanometers, Robert. Stay in your little paradise if you want, surrounded by chips. Me, I need to see normal people."

In time, the economy picked up again. Many high-tech specialists came back, attracted once more by the climate and by opportunities at new companies, like the one Mark Harris was running. The State counted on us to restore sheen to the tattered image of Silicon Valley, and to launch a new technology generation.

Nothing felt quite the same, however. Nanotronics was in danger of following the example of companies destroyed by the bubble, blown apart by hype and unrealistic expectations. Investors had turned skeptical, even sour. All our claims of technical breakthroughs and great discoveries that we were keeping under wraps prior to patenting them failed to impress people. Hadn't a Stanford physicist, a semiconductor expert, stated in the pages of *Chipworld* that our theories were wrong and that our claims about manufacturing the B-7 were impractical, bordering on fraud?

The elevator door opened at the cleanroom level. I found myself face to face with Linda Levinson, our production manager. She was coming out of the ion implanter air-lock, pulling off her green suit and plastic booties. In a semiconductor plant where the slightest particle of dust is banned, it is hard to tell men from women: both are encased in shapeless technical suits, their heads in bags that imprison their hair, faces hidden behind thick safety glasses.

Once freed from her translucent wrappings, Linda regained her human identity as a tall brunette in jeans. Behind her, through the yellow glass, I could see robots lined up for hundreds of feet. Their blinking lights indicated the state of production, latency, or calibration. Technicians moved around the machines like fat insects, ensconced in their shells: red for operators, yellow for maintenance, green for supervisory personnel. Two lasers the size of locomotives occupied one side of the room.

Linda joined me in the elevator, punching the already-lit button for the boardroom floor. She had forgotten to take off her glasses, and her eyes were ill-defined spots. She lifted a transparent, cylindrical box up towards me in an enthusiastic gesture, but did not offer to let me scrutinize its contents. I couldn't have analyzed it anyway, and she knew it. I wasn't a scientist. My background was in linguistics, history, and finance and I had come to Silicon Valley only through a series of random episodes headhunters liked to call "opportunities." Susan would have said I'd been seduced by the absurd salaries startups offered during the technology bubble. She'd probably have been right. The bubble had burst; my salary had been divided by three. My economic survival was due to a long friendship with Mark Harris, who needed a realistic associate: I could put precise

10

dollar figures on the dubious dreams of engineers carried away by their technical visions. He said I was his stabilizer.

The elevator reached the top level, not without a final attempt on the part of the publicity screen to sell us a Chevy. I let Linda get out first. We stepped into the large room where Mark Harris waited for us.

Mark Harris hadn't made it to the top levels of finance without cutting a few corners. Nothing illegal, yet his ascension had been characterized by a series of abrupt decisions that left a bitter taste in the mouths of former partners, jettisoned without much regard for their welfare. He was three years younger than me. He wasn't tall, or handsome, but he impressed his peers by projecting creativity and power, dominating any meeting. He held the floor because he always knew the fine details of every case. He had a unique way of reframing basic data into a form that suggested novel solutions. He often came up with new frameworks that had eluded his collaborators.

So much for his talents. Yet he wasn't the same Mark Harris I had known at the University of Chicago, where he studied math and engineering while I attended business school. We had met at the rowing club, where our intense training sessions on Lake Michigan had resulted in a strong bond of friendship. Even then he displayed that endurance, that ability to focus on a single task, that was to serve him so well in business; but he also knew how to have fun, to come up with practical jokes at the expense of a teacher or a fellow student after a few beers at the corner bar.

Mark Harris, senior partner at Harris & Preston (the top investment bank in San Francisco), had taken control of Nanotronics after a brutal confrontation with the founders when the company was skirting with bankruptcy. He had managed to stabilize it by demanding prodigious efforts from the few engineers who survived the massive headcount reductions he instituted. He had paid the price in his personal life. His doctor kept telling him to go on vacation. Mark agreed with the idea, and he spoke of plans to go away for a couple of weeks for a change of scenery— once pressing technical issues were resolved. He spoke of sailing in Brazil. But there were always new issues to resolve, and he spent endless hours at the office. His family life took the hit. A vicious circle.

I was familiar with the problem. I knew the signs from my breakup with Susan. But our own parting had been simple, as we didn't have any kids. Mark's wife was a beautiful blonde named Cheryl. I had introduced them to each other back in Chicago days when she was a journalism student at Northwestern. He had fallen madly in love with her. They had a 12-year old son named Ricky.

During the week, Mark rented an executive suite with a kitchenette in a nearby hotel. He only saw his son on week-ends, when he got home exhausted, a bundle of files under his arm. One evening, he'd confided to me that Cheryl had consulted an attorney at a firm that specialized in divorces.

Mark motioned for us to take our seats around the board table. Linda handed over the cylindrical box. John Brannan, our top technical expert, sat to Mark's right, and our treasurer to his left. An attorney from the firm of Wilson Sonsini arrived, followed by a young paralegal who carried a fat briefcase. They sat near me, along with George Preston, Mark's partner, a man with graying temples, ten years his senior. George was a quiet financier, a Wall Street banker type. Thanks to his international contacts, he had convinced the Goldenstar Fund to put a few million in our coffers. He had a mustache, wore gold-rimmed glasses, and kept his impeccable jacket on while the rest of us, even the lawyers, were tie-less and in shirtsleeves.

The wide windows looked out on San Francisco bay, framing sailboats lined up in the marina and airplanes on final approach to the airport. The sun was already high in the sky.

Mark opened the box Linda had brought him. His fingers were trembling. He realized it and gave a dry laugh. "I drink too much coffee," he said, setting down the plastic lid. The box contained a stack of iridescent disks, larger than DVDs and twice as thick. He picked one up, holding it by the edges, and lifted it for all to see. There was a moment of silence, of intense attention, as if we were at Mass when the priest holds up the sacred host. I almost expected to hear a bell. Mark could have said: "This is my flesh."

"A new technology is born! The first B-7 wafer."

We held our breath. Mark turned to John Brannan.

"We have all the calibrated results, right?"

Brannan pointed to a lab notebook in front of him. He opened it so we could see the graphs, the measurements signed by every technician, authenticated by Linda and him, complete with the dates and the times of measurements. He showed it to the attorneys. The guy from Wilson Sonsini requested copies. He said a few words to his assistant, who was taking notes.

"Naturally, there's still a lot of work ahead of us!" said Linda Levinson.

She had taken off her glasses. Her blue eyes sparkled. It's not every day that one brings a revolutionary technology out of the lab!

"What you have in front of you is the seven-inch wafer. In order to get to mass production, we need to scale up the diameter — without compromising quality — to ten inches or even twelve. Only experiments can tell us whether or not that's possible."

"Those developments are anticipated in our plans, and also in the budget," noted the treasurer with a satisfied air. "The first orders are coming in fast."

I felt swept away by their enthusiasm, tempered only by the fact that our cash reserves were almost exhausted, no matter what the treasurer said. I raised my hand.

"Robert? What do you think?"

"Okay, so we've got proof of concept. The B-7 wafer exists. That's a huge step. Next we setup volume production, the slicing, dicing, polishing, that's all under control. But let's be realistic. For this to fly, we need to ramp up sales — and that takes money. Lots and lots of money. It's time we planned the initial public offering."

"Then we do agree," said Mark, turning toward the lawyers. "You'll draft a notice to the Securities and Exchange commission, right?"

"The standard notice for preliminary filing, Mr. Harris. It'll be ready this afternoon. We can start drafting the prospectus. That will take the most time. We must have all the technical data, the patent applications, the risk disclosures."

"You've got all powers," said George Preston, his tone quiet in contrast to the excitement simmering around the table. "Do whatever you guys have to do; just make sure we're all very wealthy in a few weeks!"

Laughter broke the tension. Mark gestured at someone beyond the glass separating us from the offices. He had planned everything. His secretary came in, smiling, holding a tray with glasses and a chilled bottle of Champagne. John Brannan got up to write a few figures in red on the white board. I read:

- Top Nasdaq scenario: $ 350 million, IPO in September.
- Backup scenario: $ 300 million, with lock-up.

Engineers had their technical jargon, full of expressions like differential rotation or ionic density. Businessmen spoke lovingly of their IPOs, their "initial public offerings," which, in the end, amounted to a pile of dollars.

What would Susan think if she saw us, a glass of Champagne in one hand, a pen in the other, building up these complicated schemes to accumulate wealth through a technical house of cards, always " pushing the envelope," as NASA astronauts liked to say? She would poke fun at us, yet she'd be wrong, because companies like

14

Nanotronics were changing the world, launching new products that moved the economy forward and created jobs.

"At what price? What sacrifices?" Susan would demand to know.

I didn't want to have to answer.

Mark raised his hand to get our attention.

"We'll have to set up a committee, to set the share price. Can you chair it, George? With Robert? And Dr. Brannan?"

"When did you start calling me 'Doctor'?" asked Brannan.

He was a tall, dry fellow with a balding forehead. He wore his University ring: a huge fake stone, an emerald.

"Ever since you started billing me $2,000 a day for your time! Not counting your stock options!"

Everyone got up, laughing. I drained my plastic glass, enjoying the last bubbly gulp. Mark's secretary went around picking up papers. She carefully erased the white board. Linda went off with George and the attorneys. I remained in the room with John Brannan and Mark. With the same motion, in silence, we walked over to the window to stare at the shoreline of the bay.

Mark had kept the wafer. Under the rays of the sun it was beautiful. It threw off rainbows. I could see the outline of chips that robots would have to cut, very precisely. Other robots would mount them over special substrates. Linda had said it: there was a lot of work ahead. The feeling of euphoria dissipated. We looked at the disk with a more critical sense.

"The key element here is system performance, as we scale up to mass production," said Mark, facing John Brannan. "Do you think we have the right team to do it?"

John didn't answer right away. Still holding the lab notebook, he opened it at random and ran his fingers over the graphs as if seeing them for the first time.

"It's a huge challenge. We'll have to climb up the power curve, all the time sticking to basic standards. This wafer is only a prototype. On the other hand, Nanotronics has some excellent engineers. Linda Levinson is remarkable."

He could not resist adding: "Not to flatter myself, but I believe I've given them some good advice."

Mark turned to the window, his eyes sweeping the wide landscape.

"I'm worried about competition. Samsung, to begin with. Huawei. And the Taiwanese. We need to move very fast. Nobody has ever put on the market a product with that computational speed, combined with these communication characteristics. But they will try."

Brannan remained silent, swaying from one foot to the other like a kid.

"Precisely. Our system may be too powerful for today's market. It makes possible some modes of remote detection for which there isn't a ready application yet."

"You hadn't told me that!" Mark seemed taken aback.

"I wasn't sure, until we ran the experiments last night. Here it is, if you must know: there's a secondary mode where the system emits outside of the electromagnetic regions commonly defined by Maxwell's equations."

"An undetectable signal? Then it's useless."

"It's useless, yes — for the time being. I call it the stealth mode."

"What if we kept it to ourselves? Used it as a secret weapon against competition, when it comes."

"Without patenting it? Our lawyers will never agree."

"To hell with the lawyers! They'll be busy enough with the primary applications; and the public offering."

"What about Goldenstar, our investors?"

"No reason to bring them into this."

John Brannan shrugged, spread his arms: "You're the boss. If you want to keep it secret, I won't object."

Mark turned to me.

"What about you, Robert? I worry, when you don't say anything."

16

I took the wafer from him. I watched the colors slide off its surface, as if it was a crystal ball about to reveal the future.

"We shouldn't put a product on the market ahead of practical applications," I said — a statement straight out of first-year business school. "Emitting a signal nobody can detect... As you said, that's pointless. Nanotronics should introduce this product with a solid base of well-recognized applications, while continuing to research this stealth mode discreetly, looking for more advanced capabilities."

"That's wise advice," said John. "That's what Intel would do."

That last remark carried the day with Mark Harris. Any young technology company aspires to behave like Intel.

Our fate was sealed that day. We couldn't anticipate the consequences of that decision.

A sailboat was leaving the harbor. It moved slowly along the channel to San Francisco Bay. I pointed it out to Mark.

"You don't have any more excuses to postpone your vacation. It'll take three weeks for the attorneys to assemble all the legal stuff. You'll get back in time to sign the papers."

"It's already decided," Mark answered quietly. "I've packed my suitcase."

I could only react with a skeptical laugh.

"Yes! The proof is, I've even called Cheryl to discuss it. She's supposed to bring me Ricky this morning. I'll take the kid with me, if she hasn't changed her mind since yesterday."

"Then I hope she'll agree, because you're exhausted, my friend. You look like death. If we're going to face Wall Street next month, Nanotronics needs a boss who's in good shape."

He said again: "I keep telling you, it's all set. It's an old dream of mine, since our days racing on the lake in Chicago."

"Are you really going off to Brazil, Mark?" asked John. "If you want sailing, you could stay in San Francisco. I've got friends at the Yacht Club. The regatta organized by Crédit Suisse starts next month."

"No thanks! I'd end up with other businessmen, who'd talk endlessly about their stock portfolios and new BMWs! Can you see me, stuck with those guys on some tiny cockle-shell? No, I need to breathe a different air, some place where the phone won't ring."

He turned to me: "What about coming along, Robert? Like the old days? You've got sailing experience. That'd be good for Ricky."

The idea made me laugh: "Three men in a boat, eh?"

He answered me in a relaxed tone: "There'll be more than three of us. I've gotten some information: we can hire a sailboat in Belèm, with a Brazilian crew, local guys who know the river. You'll see, it'll be great!"

Suddenly, the idea didn't appear so incongruous to me. Mark Harris caught you unawares like this, with notions that emerged fresh from his own brain, and he managed to convince you. I almost started to believe it had been my idea to go along.

"Tell me, what can you fish for in the Amazon?" I asked.

"You can fish for everything!" Mark replied with enthusiasm. "They have a kind of catfish that measures over three feet, and an incredible variety of species. I've read an article about a woman biologist…"

I wasn't listening to him anymore. Images from the elevator display were racing through my mind: ecological holidays in Borneo, or sailing up the Amazon with my best friend and a 12-year old kid who'd never seen a boat? That would be a great adventure. I hadn't had a real vacation for how long? I had to think hard to remember: two and a half years, maybe more — since Susan's departure. So I accepted.

Music trilled: the first bars of the Fifth Symphony. That always irritated me. If Beethoven had known he was composing ringtones for mobile phones, he could have saved himself the trouble of writing them for huge orchestras. Mark stared at the tiny screen of his digital assistant at some text scrolling by.

"It's a message from Cheryl," he said. "The car will be downstairs in a few minutes."

The Mercedes was parked in front of the lobby, under the sign that read "NO PARKING." When Mark and I came out, the chauffeur opened the back door for Cheryl. She was still blond, but her hairdresser had lightened the color even more so the sun made a golden halo around her head. Ricky opened the other door. He came out with his backpack and a digital camera.

The child had blond hair, like his mother. She had dressed him up in beige trousers and a blazer. He looked like a proper English pupil lost in the Far West.

Without acknowledging my presence, Cheryl faced Mark and said coldly:

"His suitcase is in the trunk."

As the chauffeur prepared to lift it out, Mark stopped him.

"I'll take care of it."

"His medication is in the backpack."

Ricky turned to his father with a wry face. Cheryl went on:

"I don't feel right, about this trip. You remember what Dr. Spencer said. I know you've got your rights, but…"

Doctor Spencer wasn't a real physician, but a New Age therapist who treated his women patients' anguish with extracts from plants, crystals and copper bracelets.

"You're worried over nothing, Cheryl. I'll take good care of him."

Cheryl gathered the child in her arms. He vanished among the folds of her cape. "You know what I told you. Call me if you need anything."

Ricky managed to extract himself from the maternal embrace, looking confused. He brandished his camera:

19

"Can I take a picture of you guys?"

Mark took two steps forward to place himself next to Cheryl, without touching her, standing stiffly. The chauffeur, cap in hand, was the only one who smiled.

After the picture, Mark lost no time in picking up Ricky's suitcase, saying, "Shall we go? My car's on the other side."

The kid put away his camera and waved goodbye to his mother. The Mercedes surged towards San Francisco. A sudden feeling of freedom swept over me, a sense of lightness. As if I was already on vacation.

2

Some places on Earth hardly lend themselves to cartography. They make a mockery of any attempt to frame them into maps or models. Such is the case with the Amazon basin. You can read all the brochures you want, watch video documentaries, listen to tourists talking about their adventures; but once you get there, the scene grabs you with its sheer size and complexity.

It began right at the airport. Manaus. Our plane made a wide turn above the river before landing. Once the door opened, the heat engulfed us, torrid and sticky, without any equivalent in my traveling experience. In a few minutes, I was drenched with sweat.

I recall the terminal building as an immense hangar crudely illuminated by fluorescent lamps, filled with colorful crowds. People spoke, called out to one another in a jumble of accents. It was as bewildering as a big fair, or a battlefield. A huge window filled one entire face of the building, the merest pane of glass separating us from the sweltering Brazilian night. A loud, continuous crackling sound — like radio jamming — emanated from it, accompanied by brief flashes like lightning. I watched it for a while before realizing that the noise and sparks were caused by thousands of insects attacking the glass in an attempt to reach our lights. They were insane; they hit the window and bounced off like hail in a storm. They returned again and again. Was this to be our vacation, venturing out among these savage flying insects willing to sacrifice all just to be close to the burning light and our warm blood? Our travel agency hadn't mentioned we'd be playing host to starving swarms.

In the restroom I saw an insect on the white wall. I jumped in surprise, in horrified admiration. It was a butterfly, or rather a giant moth, utterly black, as large as my two hands, with three-inch antennae. It was motionless, magnificent, and harmless. Yet I was afraid of it, as if it were about to jump off the wall and cover my face with its velvet wings, darker than the equatorial night.

Ricky and Mark Harris, waiting for me at the baggage claim carousel, had seen the insects too. We asked a passing policeman the way to the local flight terminal, where we were supposed to catch a Cruzeiro Company plane to Belèm. We were relieved to learn we could reach it through a long underground hallway, without stepping outside.

Three hours later the aircraft had taken us up the Parà River, which joins the Amazon delta. We landed without incident. A cab took us to our hotel. Here again, our impressions betrayed us. On the map we had seen Belèm as a secondary town, of reduced proportions compared to Manaus. The taxi had been driving for half an hour before I realized that the city held three times more people than San Francisco. The heat had not gone down, and the humidity remained high. You just couldn't escape it.

We had no interest in dinner. I stayed under the shower for a long time before finally sliding under the mosquito net hanging over the bed.

Among the three of us, the boy adapted most quickly to local conditions. Our sailboat had hardly left the shores of Colares Island when Ricky, barefoot and dressed only in shorts and a T-shirt, was on deck watching every move made by the two Brazilians who served as our crew and guides. He had unfolded a map of the river. I lent him my compass. He took a reading of the sun's position.

"It's very deep here. We could start fishing," he said.

Mark stayed under the tarp that sheltered the cabin. He motioned towards the man who held the rudder: "I've asked Manuel to take us to the other side of the island. Stay in the shade with me. We can fish this evening. Did you put your sunblock on? Your mom will kill me if you get sunburned." He chuckled humorlessly.

"It will be cooler?"

"Don't count on it. We're under the equator. Remind me to buy some mineral water at the cantina."

"They don't call it a cantina in Brazil, Daddy. They say, a bodega."

Manuel had heard the exchange. He smiled, revealing yellow teeth, crenellated like the ramparts of a medieval castle.

"You have a smart boy here, senhor Harris."

"What's that light?" asked Ricky.

I followed his gaze and caught a stirring in the water, a shimmering glow that spread over the river, moving upstream. As early as Roman antiquity, sailors often reported phosphorescent shapes at sea. Nowadays such lights are known to be emitted by a peculiar type of plankton, a tiny animal that becomes luminous under the right conditions.

The sky had grown dark and the weather became even heavier. Our guides, bare-chested, were covered with sweat, while we suffocated under our white fabric shelter.

Though we had set sail under a blue sky, something had changed suddenly in the atmosphere. No one in the harbor had alluded to a possible storm. A flash of lightning shook the boat. I thought I could see a circle of light in the river, probably a reflection from the stormy sky. I stepped out on deck to watch the clouds.

"If only it would rain!" said Mark, wiping his brow.

The sky had turned leaden, with filigrees of silver; cloud banks were superimposed atop one another like the bulbs of a Russian cathedral. The whole thing was bathed in a heavy, reddish light that suggested the end of the world. We couldn't even see the shores of Colares.

Not only had the weather grown increasingly warm and humid, but waves now shook us with paradoxical vortices, despite the lack of wind. The boat plunged along a 15-foot rolling flow. Blue lightning flashed. I could have sworn it came from the water below us. One of the Brazilians made the sign of the Cross.

At that precise moment, Mark's cell phone rang. He had thought that this trip to the end of the Americas would place him beyond the demands of his office. Unfortunately, Brazilian telecom services were up and running. They could find him, even in the middle of a river 40 miles wide.

"George, is that you? Say again? I missed it." He turned to me. "It's Preston. I've got to talk to him." He turned back to the phone. "Goldenstar? What do they want now?"

Ricky cast a reproachful, almost contemptuous look at his father. I would have given anything to be somewhere else.

The scene took me back to my own childhood, when my father would go away on business trips, always working on technical projects, to return weeks or months later. He worked at NASA, for the love of science, until he burned out for some reason I never learned. I suppose the bureaucracy, all that red tape, had drained away his energy. After that he was only fit for early retirement. He went to live in the hills of northern California, alone, in the fog of the North coast, beaten by cold waves.

He had wanted me to become an engineer. I chose instead to study history.

Mark was walking around the deck, cell phone in hand.

"Schedule a meeting with them when I get back, if you want. Yes, all right, all right! I'll talk to them. Just tell them to leave me the hell alone till then!"

He ended the call and looked at me as if to say, "You see, the job demands it." He spoke again, "It was George Preston. The Goldenstar Fund is furious. They demand a complete briefing on the technical aspects of the product. If I don't do it, they'll drop us. We can't get out of it."

"If you want, I'll talk to them."

But I knew all too well that it was Mark they wanted. It was his head on the chopping block.

He placed a hand on his son's shoulder as a pointless apology, with enormous tiredness. The child had refolded the map, and he returned the compass to me without a word. The boat bobbed on another swell but the blue lights did not reappear. The sky looked a bit more peaceful. The Brazilians sailed into a bay where we could find shelter until the bad weather passed.

Palm trees bordered the shoreline. We tried to sleep through the heat, but mosquitoes waged war on us and won. In the dune area we found a cabin Mark called a "bungalow." Some distance away there were a few inhabited huts. People sold us some mineral water in plastic containers. We languished about, finding it too hot to think. From time to time, one of us would get up and dive into the river.

I looked at Ricky's map again in another attempt to understand the scale of our environment. The mouth of the Amazon encompassed an island 150 miles wide. In certain places the water level could vary by 200 feet from one season to the next. I stopped trying to compare these findings with my past experiences.

Later in the afternoon Manuel came walking towards us, his fishing equipment in hand. He had on shorts and sandals.

"I had a dream," said Ricky, shaking the sand out of his T-shirt. "War broke out. I was afraid. Mom came and picked me up."

Mark rose without a word. He lifted the bag with the water bottles and some fruit and went towards the boat. The other Brazilian, Jose Batista, joined us at his own quiet pace. A dozen boys had come out of the dunes to watch us.

Even in late afternoon the air remained hot and humid. My head pounded.

"Some people can adapt to this climate. I don't think I could, even if I stayed here two years…"

"I left the aspirin on the boat," said Mark. "I could use some."

Jose Batista pushed the bark into the river. He waded in to guide it, splashing us, and jumped aboard. Manuel maneuvered to take advantage of the wind. I hoisted the little sail. As we picked up speed, the air felt a bit cooler. Ricky seemed to have shaken his bad dream. He pulled out his camera to take a picture of the line of palm trees in the distance. The sun had begun to set, and red and purple blotches appeared over the clouds and the river.

"What's amazing is that you'd think we could see the other shore," said Mark. "But it's so wide here … wider than Lake Michigan."

"And night falls so fast! I'd hoped we'd have a few hours of light still ahead of us."

The two Brazilians seemed as puzzled as we were by the spreading shadows. They stared at the darkening sky. The sun had turned to a bloody ovoid that stretched over the horizon.

Jose Batista lit a lantern; he hoisted it by rope to the top of the mast. The wind picked up so powerfully that Manuel, who held the rudder, had trouble keeping the boat on course. A furious wave swept across the whole width of the deck.

"We ought to go home, senhor. Fish tomorrow, better weather."

Mark didn't answer. He was holding onto the ropes while another squall beat down on us, covering us with foam.

"Ricky! Stay close to me!"

Jose Batista grabbed the medal he wore around his neck and kissed it. I brought down the sail but the boat kept speeding, shaken by waves, thrown this way and that by increasingly dangerous walls of water.

Suddenly a light appeared inside the river. There was no question of phosphorescence. It was the size of a Boeing, with illuminated portholes, or landing lights. It rose towards us, casting flaming reflections about the river, limning every black wave in ruby red.

In spite of the pitch and roll of the boat, Ricky found the presence of mind to snap pictures. Our small boat started to vibrate, faster and faster, as if it were about to explode. The rudder was now useless. Jose Batista knelt on the slippery deck and prayed, his face drenched with water or with tears.

The luminous craft erupted from the river with a shower of cataracts. It hovered some thirty feet overhead, surrounded by varicolored lights, laser hues that blinded us with their intensity. The craft must have measured two thousand feet across. Fat drops of water rained down on us, along with drops of light.

"Ricky!" Mark shouted from behind me in the darkness.

"I'm right here!" The child's voice betrayed his terror.

The craft began to turn, and as it did, another wave swept over us. Then I saw the black surface of its polished carapace. Suspended between us and the turbulent clouds, it reminded me of the horrible moth at Manaus airport, all shiny with strangeness.

An even more violent wave threw me against the pillar of the rudder. I grabbed it with all my strength, spitting dirty water. We couldn't see the sun any more, nor the light of the lantern. The storm had wrenched away what was left of our sail, which I hadn't had time to fold away. Tattered pieces of it were strewn all over the deck.

At that point we saw the second craft. It rose from the river depths like the first one. Moving even faster, it emerged in a vortex of such force that we spun around, engulfed by a whirlpool, without any chance of saving the boat.

I lost my hold on the pillar when the hull broke into pieces. Mark screamed in anger, or despair, and I saw Ricky swept away by an even higher wave. The river carried away the fragments of our boat. I could see them floating away in the glow of the two craft that hovered silently above us. I started swimming towards where I had last seen Ricky. I grabbed a piece of wood, part of the mast. I heard the child calling for help. I swam harder. Mark answered. In a flash, I saw Manuel climbing on top of a jagged section of the overturned hull. He was calling to his friend in Portuguese. No one answered.

"Ricky!"

The waves rose even higher. I went under, dizzy, sinking deeper until my lungs filled with water and foam. Above us, the two craft started revolving slowly, with incomprehensible majesty, exchanging signals like two aircraft carriers on maneuvers. They rose up into the black sky in a rush of energy that displaced mountains of water. I felt a body gliding near me. My hand grazed Ricky's head. I tried to grab him by the hair but a shock separated us and a heavy board hit me before I could call out to Mark, to tell him his son was drowning.

3

Human shapes were moving around me. They stopped. I caught sight of a white ceiling. The smell of disinfectant filled my lungs. I felt nauseous. People spoke to me in an unknown language. A hand passed a wet cloth over my face.

I woke up again. My vision was blurry but I was able to see the pale glow of a window; again, the white ceiling. It must be just before dawn. I couldn't move my arms or my legs. Drops fell regularly from a bottle of some liquid, hanging from a hook on a metal stand above me.

I had a dream about my father.

I had gone to see him at his office at NASA. Behind him, rocket models lined a bookcase, along with a dedicated photograph of Gordon Cooper in his test pilot suit. I was about to explain to him that Susan had left me, but what I told him had nothing to do with the impending divorce. I ended up scribbling something on a piece of paper. He didn't understand what I meant. The phone rang. Irritated, he picked it up and brushed me away with a wave of his hand.

It was daylight when I woke up again. A young bearded man in a white smock was sitting next to my bed. He spoke to me in English:

"You're lucky. They fished you out in time. "

"What about the others?"

"Your compatriot, Senhor Mark Harris, has already been flown back to the U.S."

"When can I get out?"

"We keep you for a few more days. You are at Fortaleza Central Hospital. You were evacuated by helicopter, a week ago."

"I can't move my legs."

He made a reassuring gesture.

"We'll change your bandages tomorrow. Your wounds are almost healed. Get some rest. You've lost a lot of blood."

I was too weak and disoriented to ask more questions.

I woke up again when a nurse came to replace the bottle. She gave me something to drink, a green potion with a metallic taste. In the next room a radio was playing a loud tune, a samba.

The next day, a commercial attaché from the Rio consulate came over. He gave me some news of Mark. My recovery was fully paid for. I would be flown home after a few rounds of physical therapy for my legs, in a week or so. I saw myself in a mirror. I thought about Ricky and cried.

Nothing seemed right when I got back to California. Bumper-to-bumper traffic, the animated rush of commerce. People seemed superficial, cardboard cutouts of humanity. My neighbors in Palo Alto tried to cheer me up. They called out, "Hey Robert, you're doing a good job with that cane! In a few days you'll be just fine!"

They had cut the grass in front of my house and picked up the mail piled at my doorstep. I was too shaken to thank them. It took a big effort for me to go back to Nanotronics, knowing I'd see Mark Harris again and I wouldn't know what to tell him.

George Preston knew about my return. He was waiting for me by the receptionist's desk. Good old George, a true standard of calm, with his tie, his jacket, his eternal mustache! He took me by the arm, said all the right words.

"Mark is still in a state of shock, naturally. He uses my office now. I'm counting on you to help him recover."

Some psychologist must have advised him to enlist my services, to give me the feeling I was useful. I did feel new warmth around me. There were flowers on my desk, and a card signed by all the employees. It was a folding card with a printed message. I had to hide tears of frustration, thinking I wouldn't be of very much help to Mark if I didn't regain my composure.

He was sitting next to Preston's desk, a pile of folders in his lap. George had adopted the old principle that "work is the best therapy." It didn't seem to be working. Mark was staring out the window, following an airplane. George was pressing him:

"Nanotronics is ready to go public, my friend! Thanks to you. It's your accomplishment."

"Yeah? Really?"

"There are a lot of details to work out, starting with employee stock options…"

Mark turned his eyes away from the Boeing.

"George, I just can't get my mind around this stuff — the rich getting richer …"

A technician knocked on the door frame. "Sorry to bother you, but we've got the video link with Europe. As you requested."

"The Goldenstar Fund," said George. "Very good. It's five o'clock over there. In the evening."

The technician pulled open the shiny wooden panels that concealed the flat video screen, the orientable bracket-mounted camera, and the directional microphone that he pointed towards us.

"I don't know what to tell them," said Mark, beginning to rise and leave the room.

"It's important! Think of all the work that's been done. Goldenstar manages billions of dollars."

"Can't you ask John Brannan?" asked Mark. "He knows that stuff."

Preston sat down next to him, looking worried, running a hand through his salt and pepper hair.

31

"Listen. You know how those people are, in the City; worse than Wall Street types. They want answers, hard numbers; and if they don't get them, they'll go blathering about what dinosaurs we've become. They'll say Harris & Preston has lost the Midas touch. Is that what you want? Now, I know what you've gone through. And Robert, too..."

Preston motioned toward me, and only then did Mark become aware of my presence in the room. He got up, took my hands in his. He looked at my cane, stunned. On the screen three people had appeared. Mark had no choice but to face the lens, as we did.

The technician plugged in the sound and left. The three figures started moving. In the foreground sat a teapot, several cups, and a plate heaped high with cookies. The scene made me hungry.

"Good evening! My name is Joost van Vaart. May I introduce my colleagues, Messrs Belden and Demichel, from our London office? I am based in Brussels myself. Can you see us all right?"

Van Vaart seemed to be about 45 years old, prematurely bald and stern. Belden was older. He had a pleasant smile, or else he was used to standing in front of a camera and looking friendly. Demichel was a young associate. He stared into the lens, ready to take notes on a laptop.

"We wish to express our condolences to Mister Harris in view of the terrible tragedy that has befallen his family."

Mark acknowledged this with a curt nod. He thanked them.

"We wish to confirm our interest in participating in the initial public offering of Nanotronics. However, we do have a few questions."

"Go right ahead," said George, adjusting his tie. "As you know, we are enthusiastic about the prospects for the company."

"What's the status of your patent applications?" asked Belden with an artful smile.

32

George Preston provided the answer while Mark remained silent. I had to make a few comments on some financial or legal points. Our interviewers appeared satisfied. I had the feeling that the teleconference, the inquiry about Nanotronics, was only a formality. What they really wanted was to find out the status of our team. During my hospital stay they must have picked up some rumors about Mark's fragile mental state following our accident. Wasn't he now completely obsessed with one thing: finding out what had killed his son?

"You see, everything went all right," said George with a sigh of relief. "We'll have Goldenstar at the opening. And if we have Goldenstar, a dozen big continental investors will jump in."

Mark shook his head as if to chase away a bad dream.

"Forgive me, I'm not fit to take care of that. It'd be better if you handled it without me."

I put a hand on his shoulder. "You did fine! It was important for them to see the three of us, to regain confidence."

"Confidence? Confidence in what? "

George jumped in quickly to calm things down. "Guys, please. I realize you've been through a terrible nightmare, but let's give it time to heal. We're family here. We all care. And we need you both."

Mark kept repeating, talking to no one in particular. "We didn't understand anything. We never knew what happened." He collapsed in a chair.

George dropped his therapeutic tone. "You went to the Brazilian police…"

"They were terrified. They looked for Ricky for two days. Since they couldn't find him, they locked up our crew, as if it was their fault."

"And the authorities?"

"They didn't know anything. Local people were afraid. They said that the *chupas*, the lights from the sky, were going to come back and kill them. That's happened before, they claim. And they're terrified of the police. Myself, I don't buy any of their stories. I just wish I knew what to believe."

"What about the Brazilian Air Force? Didn't they seem to know something?"

"They interrogated me for two days. I managed to convince them to fly over the site with a helicopter and look for signs of Ricky, but the only thing that interested them was the debris from the boat. They went over that with a fine-tooth comb. They treated me like a suspect. If I hadn't gotten our diplomats involved I'd still be over there, answering their questions. The ambassador kept me near him for several days. An American doctor took care of me."

So that was what had happened while I lay unconscious in a hospital bed in Fortaleza. The enormity of the story dawned on me. I felt a sharp pain in my leg.

"What did the ambassador tell you?"

"At first, he tried to sell me some stupid stories. He spoke about anthropology, for Christ's sake. He alluded to local customs, the spirit cults, Santeria, Candomblé — as if that could explain our accident. When he started getting phone calls from the people I'd called in New York and Washington, he understood I was going to shake heaven and earth to find out what happened to my son. A guy from Intelligence came into my room: cold, but very correct. He took plenty of notes and assured me he'd help me through his contacts. Mainly, he wanted to get his hands on the camera."

George and I looked at each other, stunned.

"What camera?"

"That's the only thing I was able to recover after the accident: Ricky's camera. It was a brand new digital underwater model, designed to float. The currents brought it in to shore. "

34

George echoed, mechanically, "The currents brought it back... You hadn't told me about that."

I could easily picture the scene: Mark, walking dejectedly along the river, trying to pick up any small trace of Ricky.

Mark, his voice breaking with emotion, said, "I didn't tell anybody. The last thing I want is to find my story on the cover of *Secrets of the World*, in every supermarket across America, as some tripe about invading Martians. Here, look. People will believe anything!"

He pulled a stack of magazines from his briefcase.

"The Extraterrestrials are lurking among us!" screamed a purple title on a green cover, adorned with oval-eyed humanoids devoid of expression. *How to defeat an alien abduction – the three vital precautions*, by Hubert Brock, international hypnotherapist.

"How can they make all this up?"

He was flipping the pages with his fingertips, as if ashamed he had bought such drivel — as if George and I had caught him with a porn magazine.

"What about the Intelligence guy?"

"I told him the truth: the camera was dead; waterproof or not, it hadn't survived the accident. It was filled with mud and dirty water. I'd thrown it away."

George Preston, clearly not satisfied, seemed about to press the matter further; but a courier arrived at that moment. He was a young fellow with a motorcycle helmet and a satchel filled with documents. He asked for Mark Harris and gave him an envelope. Mark extracted two plane tickets and turned to me.

"Two seats on a flight to Washington D.C., tomorrow at 8 A.M. Come with me to the Senate, O.K.? You'll be my witness. They won't get rid of me so easily! I haven't finished asking questions of my own."

The plane touched down at Dulles airport without incident, and by mid-afternoon a silent, air-conditioned limo had delivered us to the downtown area. Mark seemed

35

preoccupied. I respected his silence. Perhaps he was preparing for our scheduled meeting with Senator Healdsburg, one of the two senators elected by the State of California, whose political philosophy matched his own. Over the years the firm of Harris & Preston had contributed to his reelection campaigns. We had supplied experts to bolster various legal proposals that had established Healdsburg's reputation.

As usual this time of year, the weather was hot and muggy. The Capitol was serene for once, without an imminent election to agitate the media. Along the major thoroughfare that connects the city to the airport, trees were starting to turn to their autumn colors. It was easy to forget that lurking a few miles beyond this wall of foliage were offices of the major American intelligence and defense agencies, including the headquarters of the CIA and those of numerous electronics, computing and aerospace firms that benefited from the immense largesse of the federal bureaucracy.

Senator Healdsburg had an office in the Russell Building at the intersection of Delaware and Constitution avenues, close to the Capitol building to which it was linked by underground passages. An assistant waited for us in the lobby. He took charge of us as we passed the security inspection.

"The senator is looking forward to your meeting, Mr. Harris. I believe this is your first visit to the Senate? Your company has always had a determining influence over our initiatives in the economic domain...."

Mark wasn't listening to the fawning young man in dark suit and striped blue tie at his side. He was scrutinizing the gilded ornamentation, the impeccable carpet, and the portraits along the hallways.

"This is the oldest building of the Senate, isn't it?"

"A mythical place, Mr. Harris. Before it was built in 1909, our poor senators were forced to rent offices in town. The 61st Senate settled here, but you know how bureaucracies are: the administration grew so much that they had to erect a second wing, then two more buildings, so that today the Senate is spread out all over this part of the city."

We passed by the open doors of the great Caucus room, which Mark observed with some curiosity. Happy to serve as our guide, the young man pointed out the sculpted benches and the long seats with high wooden backs that resembled church pews, topped by eagles:

"All that dates from 1910," he said proudly. "The furniture has been preserved in its original state. This is where the Senate Hearings concerning the sinking of the Titanic took place in 1912, the Watergate hearings in 1974, and the contentious nomination of Judge Clarence Thomas to the Supreme Court in 1991. "

Deeper into the building, guards intercepted us again. Our guide was asked to show his ID badge which hung from a chain around his neck. Mark and I had to empty our pockets, open our briefcases and submit to a detailed inspection. Apparently the country was once again on alert following some incendiary pronouncements on an Islamic television station. We finally reached the main office hallway, more luxurious than the rest of the building. Official seals and state flags added a touch of grandeur to the scene.

If you were to ask an average American which country on Earth displayed a red star and a bear on its flag, they would likely answer Russia, or Outer Mongolia. I have always been struck by the fact that these two symbols are found on the flag of the Republic of California — as a sign of originality and independence.

Senator Healdsburg aspired to be recognized as the living incarnation of these values. He was very tall, with a receding hairline that exposed a generous slab of forehead that accentuated his patrician features. He stepped around his secretaries' desks to greet us, extending his hands and smiling.

"I welcome you with pleasure, Mr. Harris, as well as your colleague. We have much to talk about."

He turned to his assistant. "Would you kindly ask Doctor Barley and Stephanie to join us? Call Mr. Boterman, too. And for you, Mr. Harris, perhaps a cup of coffee? Or tea? The tea is excellent; the Chinese ambassador sends it to us."

The Senator's desk, framed by the American flag and the State flag, supported stacks of files. A credenza behind his chair held pictures of his wife and their kids. The walls were covered with framed pictures of Healdsburg shaking hands with the President at various events. Other photographs showed him among military officers, dressed in fatigues, climbing atop a tank, or inspecting a jet fighter. It was impossible to forget that he chaired the Armed Forces Appropriations Committee of the Senate, one of the most powerful committees in Congress.

"I see you're admiring my trophies," Healdsburg told me with a smile, "but the battle of the budget is never won! The President rewards his supporters with insane spending. It's our job to bring him back to reasonable levels — but we have our own constraints, our own projects."

He turned upon the arrival of a young woman with short hair, dressed in a dark blue suit, followed by a little old man with a goatee, a brown jacket and yellow tie, carrying a lawyer's briefcase with a gold clasp.

"My name is Stephanie Sheldon," said the young woman ahead of formal presentations by the senator. "I deal with legislative affairs."

"More precisely," interrupted the senator with a smile, "Ms. Sheldon manages all our connections with the White House and the House of Representatives. She's a living database. Professor Barley, on the other hand, is the science adviser to the Armed Forces Committee. Would you care to sit down? Ah, here comes Mr. Boterman."

38

I hadn't noticed his arrival. He was a gray man in his late forties, and he wore a blue suit with a butterfly bowtie. Giving us a curt nod, he sat down in a corner.

Tea was served from a pot engraved with the arms of the Senate. Eagles stared at us from atop the flag poles, the sculpted cornices, the gilded moulding, even the porcelain cups. Barley, his briefcase tucked between his feet, had taken a seat on the comfortable sofa. Mark and I sat next to him. Stephanie Sheldon placed herself in an armchair facing us, while Healdsburg took another one. His cup in hand, he leaned towards us.

"Welcome to Washington," he said. "You are men of business, not politicians, so I will not inflict any pointless speech upon you. We are here to work together. "

"Thank you for taking the time to see us, Senator," Mark began. "I need your help. This may seem like a personal issue, but it touches many people at every level."

Healdsburg did not react. He was drinking his tea in small gulps, intent on hearing what Mark had to say. Dr. Barley had opened his briefcase to extract a notebook filled with graph paper. Stephanie Sheldon had pulled a PDA from her handbag and was scribbling on the screen with a shiny stylus. Mark went on:

"I have reason to believe that the major nations — including the United States — are hiding the truth about unidentified objects that could pose a danger to the people of Earth."

I felt the professor jump next to me. He closed his notebook and moved to get up. Healdsburg extended a hand in a calming gesture, or perhaps a threatening one. The scholar sat down with a frown.

"Please proceed. We are listening."

Mark continued in his calmest, most precise voice. "My colleague and I were recently confronted by unexplained objects in Brazil, during a sailing trip on the Amazon river. You know our background in high tech. You can believe me when I say that no craft made on Earth compares to what we saw."

"There are classified projects," began the old scientist seated next to me.

Healdsburg appeared about to chastize him, but Mark spoke first:

"If such projects exist, and they are resulting in the loss of human life, they should be outlawed. If, on the other hand, there's no such research, it's time to open up the files concerning the sightings and tell the truth."

"You're going a little fast," replied Barley. "If there were unknown phenomena placing our citizens in danger, of course our government would take care of it."

"My son died because of these 'phenomena,' as you call them…"

"We are sorry for your loss," broke in the senator. "Please believe—"

"And you expect me to wait for some bureaucrats to take notice? I cannot believe that the Intelligence services and military haven't looked into this. I've collected a number of documents myself: similar objects have been tracked on radar all over the globe. They exist! Our pilots have fired on them. Higher-ups won't acknowledge a thing. In Brazil, our ambassador spun silly yarns about voodoo cults for my benefit. A fellow from Intelligence came to interview me, but it was a one-way street: he didn't give a damn about what happened to us. Yet we weren't dreaming. My son is dead because of the incompetence of these people."

Stephanie Sheldon, who had been making notes at a furious pace on her electronic assistant, raised her eyes from the tiny screen and said, "This is not a simple problem, Mr. Harris. You are not the first person to mention it in this office."

Dr. Barley, about to speak, changed his mind. The woman went on:

"We've made a few discreet inquiries over the last few years, naturally. Without success. Even the White House

40

seems unsure of whether any serious research is ongoing, among what people call the Black Projects."

"I recall discussing this with President Carter," added Healdsburg. "Clinton, too. His science adviser had been contacted by an influential member of the Rockefeller family. These enquiries never led anywhere."

"You have access to all the military services," said Mark, making a sweeping gesture at the photographs covering the walls of the senator's office. "You can request briefings: CIA, NSA, ONI, NRO, DIA, OSI, the three-letter guys, using *subpoena* power: 'Under the threat of sanctions...'"

"Naturally," conceded Healdsburg with a sigh. "Stephanie can confirm it. They always answer politely. They send over a young lieutenant in an impeccable uniform. He stands at attention before us and delivers a litany of lies for an hour."

"You are the chairman of the committee that controls the Pentagon budget. You can freeze their cash. You can stop the whole machine."

"That's not so simple! Do you know how many companies in California rely on the military budget? Including some firms that belong to the portfolio of Harris & Preston?"

It was a direct, non-diplomatic response. It checked Mark's momentum.   He looked around him — at the flags, the great seal of the State. Suddenly he seemed to realize where he was. In Washington, the rules were not the same as on the West Coast. Things didn't get done in the straightforward manner common in Silicon Valley.

Healdsburg allowed all that to sink in, and then continued in a more quiet voice.

"Give us some time to think about this problem. We are in contact with a few experts who could provide you with some information. We'll ask them to contact you. Right, Dr. Barley?"

"Yes, of course we will," said the old professor as if in a dream.

Mark went back on the offensive. "What reaction do you get if you push the top brass into a corner and demand an answer?"

Healdsburg shrugged. "We threw our auditors at them. We demanded their records. The General Accounting Office, as an agency of Congress, isn't under White House control. To give you just one example, back in the Clinton administration Laurance Rockefeller picked up on a persistent rumor about a spaceship crashing in Roswell, New Mexico, in 1947. Mr. Boterman took care of this particular issue."

Healdsburg turned to the man in the blue suit, who had not said a single word during the whole interview.

"Please tell Mr.Harris what happened, Mr.Boterman."

"I called the Pentagon. I told them I was working on the file of the Roswell events, under the authority of the Science Adviser to the President of the United States. I added that the financial services of Congress were undergoing an investigation."

He stopped, hesitated, looked at us, then at Stephanie Sheldon.

"Do continue," ordered Healdsburg, rising from his chair.

"They put a general on the line. He was in charge of the archives. I asked him to send me everything he had on activities at the Roswell base for a six-month period starting in July 1947."

Boterman halted again. Healdsburg motioned for him to continue.

"I hesitate to repeat his answer, Senator, in present company."

"We need the truth, Mr. Boterman. Our guests have flown all the way across the country hoping to understand what is going on here."

The man lowered his voice and said, red-faced: "The general told me to go shit in my hat."

We were walking down the Capitol tunnel on our way out of the building when a woman's voice called out to Mark. We turned around. Stephanie Sheldon quickly caught up with us. She held the strap of her bag over her shoulder like a rifle. For the moment, she had put away her inseparable electronic assistant.

"If you haven't made plans for dinner, would you care to join me? The Senate's restaurant is just around the corner."

We followed her into a lateral hallway leading to a richly appointed room where white-haired gentlemen, surrounded by visitors, already occupied many of the tables. I recognized several faces made famous by television.

"When Senators receive their constituents, they like to entertain them here, where the atmosphere is more relaxed than in some formal office."

Guests were recognizable by their awestruck expressions, finding themselves at the focus of political power. At one table, a group of students intently listened to a leader of the Democratic Party. At another, industrialists unrolled blueprints of a technical installation for the benefit of an elected official of their State.

A waiter glided silently towards us. He seemed to be part of the décor, like the red velvet of the drapes and the blue carpet.

"May I recommend the bean and potato soup?" he said, "It is a specialty of the house."

"Since the days of Senator Knute Nelson, of Minnesota, in 1903," added Stephanie. "We have our old traditions...."

We made a rapid selection. Senator Healdsburg's assistant put both hands flat on the table and looked at us. "I understand why you need to get to the bottom of this," she began. "Your lives have been changed, and nobody can tell you that these events did not take place. However, it would be dishonest not to warn you: you are entering a dangerous domain, a veritable mine field. You don't know what the obstacles are. Although I work for a powerful

Senator, I'm not able to sort out all the pieces of this puzzle."

"My business is to launch new projects," said Mark with a tone of bravado, "and to knock down obstacles one by one."

Stephanie extended her hand, touched Mark's sleeve. "When it comes to technology, or finance, I believe you completely. However, we are talking about much more complex issues here, and they involve a different class of players. Please do not underestimate their influence."

The waiter returned with our food. The conversation halted. I took advantage of this quiet time to look around me. We sat under a large portrait of James Madison. Other Framers of the Constitution were underscored by discreet spotlights. Golden columns rose towards drapes with elaborate fringes. I couldn't hold back a smile when I saw all the eagles, here again, clasping the folds of the velvet while they surveyed the scene below, watching us from their august perches.

"I do understand the complexity of the issue," said Mark with an assurance I hardly shared. "Since what happened in Brazil, Robert and I have been gathering up books; we've done research over the Internet…"

"Everything you've culled from current literature is likely biased," said Stephanie, "written by people who hide behind various interest groups. They have no qualms about infiltrating amateur organizations to exploit their fantasies. Ever hear of Paul Bennewitz?"

We looked at each other. Neither Mark nor I had ever heard the name. As we began tasting the excellent soup, Stephanie lowered her voice and continued.

"He was a physicist living in Albuquerque, very close to Kirtland Air Force Base, where a large number of nuclear weapons are stored. Naturally, security is heavy. The base is used as a test site for classified projects. Bennewitz, who was supplying special sensors to the Air Force, started observing luminous objects flying over the area at night. He tried to get the military to take notice, but his enquiries only called him to the attention of the counter-intelligence folks."

"What does that have to do with us?" asked Mark. "We have no interest in new weapons, or what this man observed; I only want to understand what happened to my son. What I'm looking for is the truth about the craft we saw ourselves."

"Wait a minute. Bennewitz was also looking for the truth about what he saw. He observed these things night after night, and he wanted to know what they were! Unfortunately, as it turned out, he didn't realize that the increasingly sophisticated instruments he was developing to analyze the lights ran the risk of uncovering secret experiments that had nothing to do with the phenomenon."

"I just want to understand—."

"Bennewitz, too! He was so passionate about it that he didn't listen to his military contacts when they tried to tell him to drop it because he was treading on dangerous ground. He started seeing invaders everywhere. He became convinced the military was keeping him in the dark about an imminent invasion by extraterrestrials, not about electromagnetic tests on the latest aircraft."

The woman seemed to know the story well. Obviously, this particular case had created ripples all the way to Washington and made a political impact. We didn't dare interrupt her recounting of the episode. We went on with our meal in silence, waiting to hear the conclusion.

"The Intelligence guys were frustrated by the whole situation. Bennewitz was thinking of nothing but saucers. He was picking up all kinds of electronic signals, real ones, coming from the base! He started talking about it to various folks. Since they couldn't cure his obsession, they decided to reinforce it. Disinformation teams were dispatched from Washington—"

"CIA?"

She shrugged, showing signs of weariness that hadn't been there before.

"Them, and others: NSA, special services of the Air Force, using one another as cover, as usual. I'm not smart enough to tell them apart! They befriended Bennewitz. They mounted an entire enterprise of lies, a scaffolding of myths for his benefit. He'd taken an interest in abductions, so they made up a series of legends that the poor physicist started believing. Ufologists the world over fell into the trap: not only did the extraterrestrials land on Earth, but they abducted women, impregnated them, created hybrid babies, conducted autopsies, kept human parts in transparent vials!"

"Who could possibly believe such cock-and-bull tales?" exploded Mark, brushing aside the story. "No intelligent person, especially someone trained in physics!"

"You're wrong, Mr. Harris. These services had plenty of money, and they knew what they were doing. They also kept moles in the various amateur groups, who introduced some variations over the belief systems some researchers already had. It was easy for the spooks to launch such ideas, and to give them credibility in the eyes of Bennewitz. There were books and documentaries. People assume that the government is hiding all sorts of things. They're not always mistaken…."

I cast an eye around the room. Deals were being proposed, handshakes sealed agreements on various projects, promises were made. The political machine was running at full speed.

"In good faith, self-styled researchers started hypnotizing real and false witnesses right and left. You can well imagine how juicy this was for the TV people. They loved every minute of it; they put it on the air. Mysterious sources provided sensational footage to them, fake documents, even alien autopsy videos. Entire files filled with reports and memos bearing the signatures of presidents Truman and

Eisenhower and seemingly authenticating the alien menace started circulating all the way to the Pentagon!"

"Yet this fellow Bennewitz was looking at something real, right? Something that happened on his doorstep. He must have realized what was going on."

The waiter came back with the check. Before Mark could intercept it, Stephanie grabbed it. "Let me pick this up, I have an account here."

After signing the paper and dismissing the man, she spoke again:

"Mr. Bennewitz's life did not end well. He'd become utterly obsessed with the stories the spooks were feeding him; they seemed to confirm his worst fears. Whenever he left his house, the counterintelligence heavies broke into the place to take pictures of his equipment, throw it off-track or plant false information. Little by little, the spooks drove him crazy. He ended up believing that the aliens had underground bases hundreds of miles away from Albuquerque, on an Indian reservation. Every weekend he'd fly his private plane to take aerial pictures, which was fine with his controllers. When he was circling those remote areas of the desert, he wasn't looking at the runways of Kirtland, in his own backyard. The technical secrets of the base were safe again, but a veritable psychosis of extraterrestrial invasion had been turned loose in the world."

"I still don't see what that has to do with us," insisted Mark.

"I wouldn't want to see you fall into a similar trap, that's all," said Stephanie Sheldon as she got up, smoothed her skirt, and threw her handbag back over her shoulder.

"You may think you're moving into brand-new uncharted territory. You should know it's a mine field, and others will exploit your every mistake."

She took a few steps on the way to the door, then turned back and pointed to the massive portrait of James Madison overlooking the room: "Two hundred years ago, this man

47

said, 'A popular government without popular information, or the means to acquire it, is but a prologue to a farce or tragedy, or both.' Think about it: There is no democracy without an informed citizenry. I wish you well in your endeavors, gentlemen."

4

Back in California, the weather had changed. Indian summer enhanced the colors of every flower and lifted peoples' moods. At Nanotronics there was renewed optimism in the air. During our Washington trip George Preston had spoken again to the Goldenstar managers and had obtained their support. The public offering was ready to go. Smiling, he greeted us in the conference room in late morning. The most recent test results were spread over the large table.

"The file of employee stock options is on your desk, Mark. The troops are counting on you. This time, I hope you'll take it seriously. You need to check the list again."

"I know," said Mark. "Work is the best therapy…. But I still don't know what happened in Brazil. Our trip back East didn't resolve anything."

"You saw Healdsburg? Is he going to help you?"

"He doesn't know much," said Mark evasively. "He only promised to put us in touch with some experts."

"Did he have his assistants with him?"

"Yes: a woman who serves as liaison to Congress, a scientist who works on military issues, and a federal accounting specialist."

"Did they ask about what you'd seen?"

"I told them what Robert and I experienced. And the investigation that followed. They could tell I was determined to go all the way."

Mark seemed to need to talk about it, even though the pain and the anguish washed over him anew each time. George went on:

"Did you tell them that Ricky had taken some pictures?"

"Of course not! I'm not even sure any photos can be recovered. Besides, like I told the Intelligence goon, I threw the camera out." He hesitated. "I kept the memory card, though. In the chaos that followed, I forgot it even existed until I got home and found it in my clothes. I managed to hide it, but it may be dead: I've tried to read it on two different computers. Nothing."

Mark's secretary stepped into the room after knocking discreetly on the door frame.

"Mr. Harris? General Crawford has arrived."

"Tell him I'll be right with him."

"I've made a reservation at Silks, as you requested."

George Preston looked surprised. "Air Force?" he asked, motioning towards the lobby.

"Perhaps he knows something," answered Mark. "He called me, said he was referred by Healdsburg. In the late sixties, Crawford supervised Project Blue Book. You know, the official investigation of unidentified flying objects. He's retired, works as a consultant. Still has an office at the Pentagon."

Mark invited me along to the restaurant. He picked up his jacket from the back of a chair. Preston stepped forward, smiling, as if to block his path to the door. "What about those stock options?"

After a pause, Mark answered in a quiet tone: "Always working, eh, George? You're right. I have to review the file. Let's discuss it after lunch."

The room was lined with golden fabric, adorned with medallions. There were no royal eagles here. The luxury was not as ostentatious as at the Senators' dining room. Credenzas held porcelain vases that would have done honor to the private collection of a sophisticated orientalist. Next

50

to every plate, ebony chopsticks were precisely lined up, held by an elegant knot. At Silks, the most discreet restaurant in San Francisco, tables were spaced far enough apart to assure confidentiality. I knew that Mark liked the place for his business lunches.

In his civilian clothes, General Crawford looked more the part of a quiet banker on his way to his golf club than a man of action, skilled in the craft of war. He had a heavy step and an untrusting eye, as if ill-at-ease in an establishment where he didn't find his usual references. A young Chinese woman glided towards us, presented three menus and moved away without a word. She returned a few minutes later to place a teapot in front of Mark.

"It looks like they know you here," said the general. "Pretty fancy."

"It's close to the Stock Exchange," Mark said apologetically.

"Never served in Asia," Crawford continued, fumbling with his chopsticks. "Four years in Frankfurt, two at Lakenheath, the rest between Washington and Wright Field."

"Wright Field?"

"Near Dayton, Ohio. Wright-Patterson Air Force Base. The Foreign Technology Division."

He recited this with a dryness that belied his appearance as a contented retiree, his old banker's demeanor.

A waiter came over, a napkin over his arm. He took our order: A Hong-Kong salad for Mark, the duck for me. The general picked the prawns with black mushrooms.

"Please bring a fork for the gentleman," Mark requested.

Crawford leaned towards him, speaking in a confidential tone. "The senator hasn't given me any details. If I understand right, you and your son had an accident in Brazil, following an aerial phenomenon?"

I watched Mark, his face tensing, his jaw locked in anger. He managed to keep his composure.

51

"A phenomenon? If you want to call it that. As for aerial, the object that wrecked our ship came out of the river."

The general tried a little joke:

"Perhaps we ought to bring in the Navy, then. Did you note any details of the ... phenomenon? "

"You mean, as the boat was sinking? As my son was drowning?"

I jumped in, trying to maintain calm. "What we saw was a manufactured craft, General. It emitted an enormous amount of light, and it had definite structure. It was round, perfectly smooth. At first, anyway."

"Did it make any sound?"

"We didn't hear any engines, if that's what you mean. Or the sound of a classic propulsion system. But there was thunder and lightning all around us, as if the object had somehow triggered a storm."

Crawford had pulled a notebook from his pocket. He started scribbling something on it. He seemed to be making a considerable effort to picture the scene in his mind.

"With the thunder, you might not have heard a mechanical sound, such as a motor. And you may have been blinded by the lightning strikes. Human perceptions...."

The conversation halted when the waiter returned. Crawford leaned back into the comfortable cushions of his armchair with its sculpted backrest, looked Mark in the eye and asked abruptly:

"During your discussions with the Brazilian military, did they ever mention their dirigibles?"

Mark was left speechless for a moment.

"Mention what?" he finally asked.

Crawford pulled a stack of photographs from his pocket. They showed dirigibles of the kind one sees flying over the stadium on Superbowl Sunday.

"They use them to maintain and calibrate their communication systems in forest areas. These are round

52

objects, or rather oval in shape, with lights on them, similar to what you're describing. When they fly high enough, you can hardly hear the propellers."

He seemed pleased with himself. I thought it would be a good idea to speak out. "A dirigible doesn't emerge from the waters of a river, as far as I know! It doesn't stir up waves big enough to capsize a boat."

"Of course not," answered Crawford, biting into a large prawn. "That's clear. You must have experienced a storm, the kind they often have down there, below the Equator. A deplorable coincidence, but that's a rational explanation."

Mark was choking. His hands shook. He had set his chopsticks down. He pushed back his plate with a violent motion.

"I won't listen to this garbage for another minute! I'm not a child, General. I've seen dirigibles. I'm up-to-date on advanced propulsion techniques, those tested over at the Ames center, and at Lockheed…"

His voice rose as he grew ever more agitated. A couple having lunch at a nearby table watched us curiously.

"I don't feel like discussing what is, or isn't, rational with you."

Mark had gotten up. His cell phone rang. The waiters stared at him disapprovingly. He pulled out the device without paying attention to them.

"George? No, you're not interrupting my lunch. I was just leaving. You'll never guess. This guy tried to convince me my son died because of a dirigible. I should have known I was wasting my time with the military."

Crawford, red-faced, gathered up his pictures. I got up to lead Mark — phone still pressed to his ear — to the exit, leaving the general in front of his prawns in black mushrooms. I saw a shadow come over Mark's face. As he put the phone back into his pocket, he said to me, "Something's happened to Cheryl."

5

I parked my car directly behind the ambulance, as best I could on the steep slope. I turned the wheels into the curb and squeezed the hand brake. We got out to the afternoon sunshine, smelling the perfume of jasmine. Maureen, Mark's secretary, was waiting for us. The ranch-style house was a sprawling construction perched on the side of the green hill. It overlooked the bay and the Tiburon peninsula. From the top of the wide steps that led down to the manicured backyard, one could see all the way to the Golden Gate Bridge. The San Francisco skyline was visible on the far shore. A Japanese gardener came over once a week to take care of the flowers and trim the bushes that might block the million-dollar view.

In the early days of their marriage, Mark and Cheryl had held cocktail parties under the trees every Sunday afternoon. Their friends, mostly stockbrokers and financial executives from Marin County, came over in shirtsleeves. They arrived with their wives, sipped chilled Chardonnay from Napa, and spoke enthusiastically of new Nasdaq record highs, or the exchange rate of the yen. After a few glasses, conversation would turn to the fate of local baseball and football teams, the Giants and the Forty-Niners, who had uneven fortunes. Susan had attended these gatherings with me, always vivacious, sure of herself, her intelligence, our future. That was before the crisis, the debacle of the investment banks. So long ago!

"The doctor is with her," Maureen said. "Her life isn't in any danger."

"Why the doctor?" inquired Mark.

"She tried to commit suicide. Come and talk to her. You too, Robert; you're a long-time friend."

As Mark didn't seem to understand the situation and walked along like an automaton, she grabbed him by the arm and added, "She'll be fine."

We found her cowering on the living room sofa. Cheryl had folded one arm to hold a cushion over her head, as if eager to hide, to avoid seeing and hearing anything. When Mark tried to uncover her face, she dug deeper into her shelter, without a word.

Standing behind the couch was "Doctor" Spencer, her New Age therapist. He was pale and seemed overwhelmed by the situation. Yet he deserved credit for calling the ambulance and securing first aid for Cheryl, whose wrists were bandaged. One of the paramedics came towards me.

"Somebody needs to sign the sheet for the emergency response. And to say you take responsibility for her care. That's you?"

I signed the document. As he was about to leave, I asked, "Did she lose a lot of blood?"

"No, she didn't know how to do it. She only sliced the skin. She panicked when she saw the result. Spencer's the one who called us."

"You know Spencer?"

He gave a wry smile. "Who doesn't? His women patients all have problems. Since he treats them all with plant extracts— Well, things seldom get better. We generally end up getting called."

His unfriendly remark seemed to have put him in good spirits. He extended a hand. "You're a friend of the family?"

"I've known them a long time. Do you have any idea why she did this?"

"None of my business, but you might want to call the cops next. Check out the bedroom at the end of the hall. That's where we found her."

Right away I knew what the paramedic meant. That was Ricky's bedroom.

I walked down the hall and stopped at the open doorway. The walls, with their posters of well-known athletes and a female rock singer with her guitar, were the only untouched part of the room. The mattress on the bed had been sliced open, drawers were overturned, the bookcase was broken and books scattered everywhere. Even a chair had been inspected, the fabric torn apart. A plastic model of a rocket, three feet long, had been ripped open and dumped in a corner.

In the living room, Cheryl was sitting up. She sipped a glass of water Maureen had offered her.

"I've given her something to calm her," said Spencer, looking at me as if I were in charge of operations.

I gave him an approving sign, in the same spirit.
Mark drew close to her. "I feel so lost, too, you know...."

She gave a pale smile that conveyed more bitterness than resignation.

"We've already discussed it," she said, trying to cut short any explanation.

"You could stay with your folks for a while; get away from this house."

"That wouldn't solve anything, Mark. This nightmare won't stop. I tried to stop it." She held out her wrists. "Here's the result. Another mistake!"

She cried again, and then reclined on the sofa, squeezing her cushion, as if ready to fall asleep. Whatever plant extract Spencer was using seemed to be having an effect. Mark raised a hand, to touch her, to soothe her—then let it fall. I led him to his son's bedroom. He started shaking when he saw the damage.

"Who would have done something like this? And why?"

The answer seemed obvious to me. "Someone who was looking for Ricky's camera. Cheryl must have caught them in the act. They haven't touched the living room, except for the desk drawer."

"We ought to call the police. Look for prints."

"You didn't have a security system?"

"They must've neutralized it."

They, whoever they were, had done methodical work. The legs of the small desk had been unscrewed. It wasn't surprising that Cheryl should have been overwhelmed with emotion when she saw her son's room in that state.

"Don't call the police. There won't be any fingerprints. This isn't the work of some petty thief looking for twenty bucks in order to buy drugs."

"Who was it, then?" asked Mark, as if imploring me to solve the problem for him on the basis of sheer intuition.

I told him, "Someone who is very interested in Brazilian dirigibles."

That left him scratching his head. Spencer came towards us, his bag hanging from his shoulder. I wondered how many little vials he was carrying, from one patient visit to the next, leaving behind worthless prescriptions and extravagant bills.

"Time to take my leave," he said, plainly relieved. "I've called Social Services for a psych follow-up."

He wasn't cut out to deal with emergencies, especially suicide attempts. His "medications" were designed to keep his patients quiet, not to help them survive life's crises.

"By the way, *Doctor*," I asked, stressing the title. "How did you find out that Mrs. Harris was in trouble?"

"I call her every Tuesday to check on her supply of Calmophrene, one of the extracts she has to take regularly. She picked up the phone, but I only heard a sort of moan. Her line stayed open. I came over as fast as I could."

"You did the right thing," said Mark. "You may have saved her life."

"You can count on me! I found your office number in her handbag."

Excusing himself, he left. I watched out the window as he got into his Jaguar. All things considered, in this world of parasites, he wasn't such a bad devil.

Maureen offered to stay by Cheryl's bedside. I took Mark to his study. The time had come to tackle the problem from scratch.

It was a magnificent room, the walls paneled in fine wood, topped with sculpted moldings. One section framed an old tapestry while the garden windows were trimmed with crimson curtains, transparent drapes and gold cords. A bookcase, set at an angle, created a secluded reading space. Behind the desk were two antique maps: one displayed the world in the days of Christopher Columbus; the other, North America as early navigators represented it. California was shown as an island, separated from the continent by the sea of Cortez. The maps, by themselves, must have cost a fortune.

Mark stood by the desk, somberly looking at his computer screen where references were lining up. His entire environment seemed to vibrate at the same rhythm while the searches he fired up under Google and Yahoo! displayed links to a few thousand Internet sites that claimed to bring some answer to the mystery of unidentified objects. The list included various California cults dedicated to the mysterious Lemurians, pseudo-scientific organizations that proposed complex analyses and hundreds of webizens who wrote about the inhabitants of various planets with whom they were in close — sometimes intimate — contact. It was a world of charlatans and crazies, punctuated by fratricidal attacks, intractable quarrels among various chapels, among which a few sincere scientists and researchers drowned in the noise.

In the kitchen, on the other side of the wall, we could hear running water and rattling pans. Maureen must be fixing a meal. Mark jumped feverishly from one website to another, hoping to uncover some new bit of information, some untainted thread of truth. He stumbled on a catalog of photographs showing saucers in vivid color, with luminous portholes and landing gear made up of multiple spheres.

"That doesn't look anything like what we saw," he commented with irritation.

"I told you that was a waste of time!"

He turned off the machine and collapsed into an armchair. I sat down next to him.

"What did you do with Ricky's chip?"

He extended a weary arm towards the California map. "Lift the frame."

I unfastened the heavy panel from the hooks that held it and put it down, uncovering a simple vault built into the wall. I asked Mark for the code: it was his date of birth. Any idiot could have guessed it.

There was no hidden treasure inside; only a single envelope containing a flat memory card the size of a postage stamp.

"Another half-hour and those intruders would have found this."

Mark ignored my remark, and the reproach it contained.

"Why haven't you done something with these photographs?"

"It's not that easy. I told you, I couldn't read them."

"There's lots of data recovery experts out there," I pointed out.

"That's not good enough. They need to be analyzed, not just printed out. We need an expert in digital imaging, someone we can trust, someone who won't go trying to sell them to *Time Magazine*."

"I do know someone," I said without thinking. "Someone we can trust."

I regretted it the moment I said it, a knee-jerk reaction to Mark's frustrated challenge. I was thinking of my father. At NASA he had been regarded as the expert on planetary images. The walls of our home were covered with magnificent prints on glossy paper: Saturn's rings, the hidden face of the Moon with its craters.... Terrestrial views, too, where areas of industrial pollution were highlighted in false color. He had invented algorithms, mathematical masks, digital smoothing routines that could extract unsuspected details from the slightest smudge on a digital image.

The only problem was that I hadn't had any contact with him in two years. He had made some painful comments to me after Susan's departure — a difficult point in my life when I wasn't able to face reality.

Mark jumped up, stimulated by my remark. I must have spoken in an authoritative tone, because he seemed convinced anew that action, any action, was possible. He wanted to meet with this famous specialist immediately.

"Let's get in the car; I'll tell you about him on the way. It's a two-hour drive along the coast. If you want to get there before nightfall, we need to start now."

I put the map back in its place. Mark knelt next to Cheryl and kissed her hair. She did not wake up. He instructed Maureen to close all the windows and showed her how to reconnect the security system. I took the envelope with the tiny chip, sliding it into my pocket. We walked over to my car.

The Golden Gate Bridge stretched before us in the late afternoon glow, filtered by a haze along the Pacific shore. We could see the San Francisco skyline in all its glory, down to the tiniest detail: a postcard view, a tribute to all the joys of a happy life.

6

At every turn in the road we saw moldy cabins, worm-eaten fences, garages filled with the rusting carcasses of old junkers. Occasionally we passed through stands of giant trees — redwoods as straight as the pillars of a cathedral. When we got closer to the ocean, we saw moisture in all its forms, as rushing waterfalls, foggy swirls along rocky cliffs, a condensing haze on the windshield, or big drops falling from tree branches.

I couldn't avoid calling my father to tell him about our plan. He answered me as if we spoke to each other every day: a normal pitch of voice, quite even, without the slightest note of surprise. "No problem, Robert, come over whenever you want. You know the way. Yeah, bring your friend, of course. You'll want something to eat?"

Such offhandedness shocked me. I'd have preferred hearing a litany of complaints. After two years, he would have had every right to scold me. "Do I count for so little with him," I wondered, "if he takes my sudden visit so casually?"

He was probably right. I was ridiculous and stupid. He may have waited for this call from me every night, alone in his sprawling house where he had installed an observatory — which couldn't have been very useful, with all the fog rolling in from the Pacific. Over ten years had passed since my mother's death. Spending too much time among his New Age friends and marginal types, my father had taken

61

an interest in astrology, in spite of all his credentials among the most prestigious scientific labs. Back when we were still cordial he had drawn up my horoscope. His conclusions turned out to be wrong.

"Let me warn you," I told Mark, his silhouette just visible as we drove into the dusk. "You're about to meet a fairly rigid man, an old egotistical scientist with a double doctorate who thinks he's some sort of prophet."

"I know the kind. I had Carl Sagan as a teacher once. And John Brannan is my technical adviser. Your father isn't likely to shock me."

After an hour on the road we reached Point Reyes where a few art galleries were still lit up, as was a bakery and a small restaurant, empty of tourists. We stopped to order some sandwiches. The stereo played a haunting song by Jolie Holland:

I've got a couple of food stamps,
And a caffeine buzz…

Local artists had hung their paintings on the walls: butterfly wings inspired abstract shapes, seascapes were displayed next to fields of flowers. For a hundred dollars you could get a naïve scene with jumping dolphins or a wide mountain vista where adventurers climbed steep cliffs while frigates braved angry waves in the distance.

North of Point Reyes, the road skirted a vertiginous bluff high above the roaring ocean. The fog rose in swirls that seemed fake, too artful, like the fanciful background of some Hollywood horror film. The road would dive towards the sea, then rise again in a series of dizzy hairpin turns towards dense forests and ramshackle hamlets, former communes abandoned by the last hippies. We plunged down towards a cove where the fog had cleared. We could see a small boat yard with rusty trestles, ancient hulls resting on their side in the sand dunes, a pontoon.

"That's Banderas Bay," I told Mark, pointing out the sailboats tossed around by the waves. "We're almost there."

"Who lives around this place?"

"People who came as simple tourists and fell in love with the area; fishing enthusiasts; also oyster producers, a few farmers. The region is very fertile, it supports orchards and nurseries. You'd also find some artists, intellectuals who've fled the city to make their home in the hills. They don't have enough stamina left in them to start again." I couldn't help adding, "Like my father."

"Is he really going to analyze Ricky's pictures in the middle of the night? Doesn't he ever sleep?"

"Haven't you seen the bumper sticker that reads, 'Astronomers do it in the dark'?"

It was good to hear him laugh.

One last turn, then the road took us towards a jumble of rocks. The house rose in defiance of the wind and the spray. My father had turned on the garage lights. I found the twisting driveway without any problem.

I was shocked by his appearance. I hadn't imagined that his hair would have turned white, and that he would let it grow so long. I didn't remember the lines chiselled into his face as if he had spent the last couple of years on some ship exposed to the sun and the salt air. He held me briefly against him and extended a hand to Mark. He noticed my limp.

"You're using a cane, nowadays?"

"That happened in Brazil. We'll tell you about it."

He turned around to pour some coffee he'd prepared for us. The room was smaller than I remembered. He'd added some pieces of furniture. There were several new desks, computers, filing cabinets, and a map of the night sky on the wall. Books were everywhere.

"It was nice to get your phone call, Robert. Why are you here on such a night? You, a Capricorn?"

There was some strain in his voice, but I answered in the same vein, "And you, with all this fog around?"

"There's more to studying the stars than looking through a telescope."

I told him about our problem, without any more preliminaries. The digital chip required no explanation. I did get tangled up in my account of Ricky's fate. Mark tried to help, recounting the storm, the ship sinking, the pictures....

Fortunately, my father took a professional approach to our story, as if we were merely consulting him on a technical matter. He connected the imaging chip to one of his computers. A few minutes later a photograph emerged. It showed three figures on the sidewalk, in front of Nanotronics.

"Who are these people?" my father asked.

It was Mark's turn to get flustered. "My son took this picture. It's my wife on the right. And our chauffeur."

A few ordinary views scrolled by: the palm trees on the Colares shore, Manuel pushing the boat, me adjusting the sail. The next nine images were stupefying. The objects we had seen over the Amazon filled the screen.

"There it is," said Mark, choking with emotion. "That thing emerged under the hull of our boat. It hovered right above us, and then it moved away, vanishing into the clouds."

"Those are outstanding images, Mr. Harris," my father said in his best professional tone. "They were taken in rapid succession. I suggest analyzing them by enhancing contours and structural details."

With the tip of a pencil he pointed at the edge of one of the objects:

"Look at these light sources. They're equidistant from each other. I'll need a little time... I want to apply a histogram to this...then a smoothing iteration...."

His voice trailed off as the images evolved on the screen. Shapes stood out now; contrasts improved, revealing some structures we hadn't seen on the evening it all happened.

My father went on working intently, forgetting our very existence. I felt the same pain that had seized me as a child when he would neglect me, carried away by one of his scientific dreams, those famous projects of his.

Two hours later he still hadn't said anything. Looking over his shoulder, we had followed with fascination how the pictures changed under the various analyses, the filters, the masks that refined them, bringing every detail into sharper focus. Finally, he stretched out his arms, relaxed his shoulders, rolled back his chair and caught us off-guard by saying, "There's only one problem with your pictures: they don't make any sense!"

It was the kind of statement he always uttered; it drove me crazy every time I heard it.

"What do you mean?" I said impatiently, pointing at the screen. "They're right here, staring you in the face!"

"They're here, but just look at these objects: their shadows, their edges, their relief…"

"So?"

"They change shape! From one exposure to the next, they're not simply spinning or moving away, they're undergoing topological transformations."

We had to admit he was right. When we looked at the details, and especially at superimposed successive images, it was clear the two craft did not maintain their geometrical integrity. In other words, not only were they moving through space, but their angles and their proportions were changing before our very eyes.

Airplanes simply did not do that. Neither did spacecraft.

"It's as if they're somehow merging with themselves," noted Mark. "As they do it, new structures seem to come into view."

"That reminds me of something," my father observed. He took a few steps towards the bookcase and extracted an old volume entitled *The Fourth Dimension*.

"I know what you're driving at," I said, anxious to head off another lecture. "In the ninetenth century this fellow Hinton was among a group of scientists fascinated by such theories. Everybody spoke of metaphysics in those days. People *of quality* got together in smoking rooms after a good dinner and joined hands to make the tables spin. They were trying to explore the Beyond, so-called spirit manifestations…. That's a bit *passé,* isn't it?"

"It's coming back in fashion," answered my father, who seemed amused. "Not because of knocking spirits, this time, but because of cosmological phenomena that remain unexplained by modern science. Haven't you heard of string theory? There must be undiscovered dimensions. The only question is whether or not they are detectable and have physical meaning. When I worked at the Jet Propulsion Lab, in Pasadena, my colleagues were looking for ways to observe them."

Mark laughed. "How funny if scientists refused to see the evidence of extra-dimensional space-time simply because they couldn't bear looking at phenomena that didn't fit their preconceptions!"

"That wouldn't be the first time, Mr. Harris. Science often takes a sudden step forward in spite of the scientists."

"Can you save these images?" Mark requested. "In this form, they're perfect."

"Give me a little more time to improve the contrast. That will make them sharper. I will save them in such a manner that nobody will be able to erase them. I haven't seen pictures like these since my time at NASA. Back then, they once loaned my services to another organization that doesn't like its name mentioned. Two of their agents had made a video—"

"A UFO?"

"Certainly not! That was a term we never heard. One would say 'some traffic' or 'a UAP'...."

"What does that stand for?"

"Unidentified Aerial Phenomenon. The military radar jockeys had an even more obscure term for them; they called them UCTs, for 'uncorrelated targets.' This way, any outside analyst would fail to find UFO cases because any keyword search under 'UFO' led nowhere. Congressional gophers who came over, in their suits and ties, armed with official instructions, never understood what was happening."

"Who was analyzing these cases? Who was doing the investigating?"

"I never knew that. These weird cases fell into a black hole. I worked hard on those images, sometimes even on signals caught by reconnaissance satellites.... I would send my results in encrypted form to another site that transferred them further. I never knew where they ended up. Most of the time it was the Navy — rather than the Air Force — that took our documents. We never saw them again. That's the kind of hypocrisy that disgusts me, that turned me off from science."

He was pacing the room, walking along the row of computer screens.

"At the end of the day, what we were doing made no sense. What's the use of having radars and jet fighters? Or spy satellites? Electromagnetic, low-observable supersonic drones? What's the use of searching for life in outer space, millions of light-years away? What if 'they' were right here, under our noses? What if there's another universe, unfolded in another dimension, five minutes ahead of us? Modern physics doesn't forbid this. Yet nobody has ever agreed that such objects might exist."

"You never spoke to me about that!" I blurted out.

"You were taking me for a tired old crackpot, bypassed by modern life. You had all the arrogance of youth."

I lifted my cane to show it to him. "I don't have the youth any more!"

"What about the arrogance?"

I couldn't come up with an answer. I brought the discussion back to the unknown objects. "You could have blown the whistle, organized some leaks, contacted the President!"

He shrugged. "You don't understand, Robert. I did try. First in private. Later I sought the help of more than one White House science adviser. They all laughed. You can't blame them; the position doesn't have the right clearances."

"You could have used public opinion, the media—"

"Ah, the media! They were thrilled by the subject, for all the wrong reasons. A bunch of zealots were camping in front of the White House with inflatable green aliens and signs protesting the Cosmic Watergate. That looked great on television.... But how many politicians want their picture taken with an inflatable Martian?"

"I wouldn't have let them off the hook so easily if I'd had the evidence."

"Ah, Robert, your old arrogance again."

"Must be in my genes."

"Haven't you learned anything?"

"Not from you. You weren't interested in teaching me."

My father and I froze, both shocked by my outburst. "Is that what you think, Robert?" my father asked. He sounded sad. He cleared his throat and turned away. "How are you, anyway? You haven't gotten married again, have you?"

The question nailed me. I should have expected it. "Why are you asking me that? I'd have told you—"

"I haven't seen you in two years. Lots of things can happen in two years. You haven't spent too much money on phone calls, either."

He moved away to reset the color printer.

"Whatever became of Susan?"

"Back to her folks, with half of the furniture. She was fed up with Silicon Valley."

He gave me an indulgent smile, but remained silent while the splendid images of the Brazilian objects were printing on large sheets of glossy paper.

Tears welling up, I had an impulse to hug him, but I had the feeling I'd already embarrassed Mark enough.

"Can we take the prints? I'd like to study them with our engineers, back at Nanotronics."

"Sure. I'll keep the digital files. I'll let you know if I discover anything else of interest."

He returned the camera chip to us, and rolled up the large prints.

"Be careful. It's unlucky to mess with that stuff."

Mark didn't reply. My father saw us to the car. He shook Mark's hand, saying, "I'm sorry about your son." He took me by the shoulders and added, "Take care of yourself."

Driving down the hill, I could see his house in the rearview mirror. Sometimes the swirls of fog made it look like a warship, at other times an austere castle.

On the trip south towards San Francisco, the precipitous drop to the ocean was on Mark's side. He watched the waves crashing on the rocks far below. At every hairpin turn he feared the car would tumble and join them. I was driving too fast, shaken by this awkward reunion with my father, who had looked much older and who stirred up too many memories. My leg hurt; braking hard on the downslopes was painful. We were stuck behind an eighteen-wheeler loaded with huge logs, on the road to some sawmill. From Northern California all the way up the Oregon coast, forests provided the long boards essential to the construction industry. They would be used to build houses in San Francisco, Sacramento, Los Angeles.

Another car was behind us; a red convertible with the top down, its tires screaming through the turn. The crazy car was blinding me with its high beams. The driver must have been insane, on drugs, or both.

"Let those idiots pass," advised Mark.

I took advantage of a long stretch with good visibility to swerve onto the shoulder. The convertible passed me by inches, kicking up dust and gravel. I had a glimpse of two men wearing leather jackets. I lost sight of their car at the next turn.

"Watch it!"

On the downslope the convertible had caught up with the logging truck. Instead of passing, the red car drew abreast of it, blocking the oncoming lane. The man in the passenger seat stood unsteadily, leaned out and grabbed the side of the rig with one hand. He got hold of the straps that secured the load. In his other hand he held some bright tool, but it wasn't clear what it was or what he was doing.

"What the hell," Mark said, intently. "They're both crazy."

As the truck entered a turn, the man let momentum throw him back into the convertible, which sped ahead in a cloud of exhaust and the stench of burned rubber.

An enormous shape rebounded on the pavement ahead of us. It seemed the whole mountain was crumbling. I slammed on the brakes, my car swerving across the road. I felt a violent shock, heard a commotion. A window had shattered, but we kept moving. More tree trunks bounded around us. They bounced up, rolled over, and blocked our lane. How I managed to avoid them, I'll never know. The half-empty truck sped away.

When the dust settled, I saw how far we had skidded: we were stopped at the very edge of the precipice. Mark had his head in his hands, his forehead bleeding from the impact of glass shards. The engine had stalled.

A delivery van that had been following a ways back slowed down and parked on the shoulder next to me. Its emergency lights blinked on.

"I saw everything!" said the driver, a heavy-set man of about sixty, wearing jeans and a T-shirt with the logo of a beer company. "They tried to kill you!"

70

I got out and shook the guy's hand. Together we inspected the car. The left rear door had a big dent and Mark's window had shattered, but the vehicle seemed able to start again.

"Your buddy's hurt." Mark waved him off.

"My name's Kramer, Tony Kramer. Don't stay here. They might come back. I know a place where you'll be safe."

I managed to get the engine restarted, and I followed Kramer's truck, trying to control my emotions. We had to drive around a few of the trees that had rolled further down the road. The little harbor of Banderas Bay appeared in my headlights. Off in the direction of San Francisco, the sky had the purple cast of approaching dawn.

Part Two

BANDERAS BAY

7

Near the shore the cool of the ocean enveloped us; musty smells rose from the bay. At the end of the pier, the light from a single lamp atop a distant mast was splintered into a thousand flashes by the rippling waves. The edge of the cove was strewn with debris. Black currents rocked a dozen ancient barks. After the rush of our insane race, this vision of the harbor seemed magical to us. In the darkness, a cat fought with some animal that fled under a parked car before burrowing behind a rotting fence. Some distance from the path, an old barn served as an oyster bar. The surrounding area was piled high with discarded shells.

The place was not as deserted as we had first imagined. The winches that secured a few boats awaiting repair appeared in working condition, and a white, modern yacht was held in a travelling-gantry crane, ready to be launched into the ocean. Propped on blocks, other hulls awaited a new coat of paint or a reconditioned engine.

The lantern swinging in the distance seemed to belong to a barge where two silhouettes were stretching some nets. Beyond piles of crates and a hangar filled with chains and mechanical parts, other dim lights provided signs of life. An entire community was resting there, ready to wake up amidst the smells of algae and mounds of oyster shells.

Kramer guided us along a well-worn path where tractors had left deep tire ruts. We reached a wooden cabin with a washed-out sign where we deciphered the word OFFICE painted in white letters. Next to it an antique panel read:

74

MARY'S CAFE – ALWAYS OPEN. We reached it by climbing over rough boards that formed three uneven steps. The redwood deck was lined with a triple row of iridescent abalone shells, a rare mollusk subject to strict fishing quotas. The owner of the place must not have been overly concerned with local laws restricting the size of the catch.

The rambling structure was perched on massive piles that plunged into the mud. When we pushed open the screen door, we faced a counter and rows of shelves loaded with fishing tackle, lures and hooks, and special tools to mend the nets. There was a cork bulletin board where local folks had pinned pictures of the boats they wanted to sell: ten thousand dollars for an outboard speedster, or forty thousand for a trawler that must have seen many an expedition to the Farallone islands or gone up along the Oregon coast in search of salmon.

"You'll find some quiet here," said Kramer. "Folks are nice. They expect you to keep your nose out of their business, but they'll treat you the same way." He offered his hand and we both shook it. "Good luck, maybe we'll see each other again. Around here, I take care of mechanical stuff, everything that moves, greasing winches, fixing cranes, pumps and wells, that's my job!"

And then Tony Kramer was gone, with no chance for us to thank him properly.

The store was lined with shelves holding all the necessities of everyday life, from hardware parts to groceries, postcards, coloring books, special tongs for crabs, batteries, T-shirts with decals of whales, camping stoves and trailer necessities. There were navigation systems, compasses and solar panels, fish knives, mapping software, nautical charts and satellite sensors. The whole selection evoked a culture of rugged individuals and old hippies, the long shadow of the Sixties and the Summer of Love, and the communes that once flourished in the region, mixed in with the waves of refugees that followed: Vietnam veterans, survivors of financial collapses, retirees from bureaucratic drudgery, losers of political fights, souls shipwrecked by religious passions, flotsam left behind by Reaganism and Bushism, brainless children of the sects and the drugs, not to mention passing tourists in Hawaiian shirts and Sunday mariners who drove up in their new SUVs.

The café area was an extension of the store onto a terrace that smelled of mud, a structure nailed together from boards that stretched over the water. There were three wooden tables with rustic benches held in place by big rusting bolts.

"We've got toast if you want. And some eggs. It's too early for fresh fruit; they won't deliver before eight."

The waitress, a tall girl in jeans, wore a leather jacket with a compass card in the back. She had magnificent eyes, a deep green. That's how she entered my life. With her eyes.

"Are you Mary?" asked Mark, pointing at the sign by the door.

She laughed freely, tossing back her head. "Mary's been gone for a long time!"

She didn't introduce herself. She continued, "Tony told me about you. Take it easy for a while. We'll take care of your car. You've still got some blood on your forehead."

She went back behind the counter. Minutes later she returned carrying a tray loaded with hot coffee, toast and jam, omelets and sausages. She also brought a wet towel she used to clean Mark's wound.

"Jimmy, go drive their car under the hangar," she told a boy who couldn't have been much over sixteen. "Walk around it to make sure it's not leaking oil or gasoline. We don't need a fire."

I gave him my keys and he walked off, as did the waitress, leaving me sitting with Mark at the edge of the blackness that dawn had yet to dispell.

Spreading the local map over the wooden table, I opened up the cardboard tube that held my father's computer prints. The phenomenon was displayed there in all its horrible splendor and power. We began eating breakfast in silence, with special appreciation for the hot coffee. Then we looked at the photographs again.

"I might as well tell you. Until that crazy truck episode on the road, I was ready to throw in the towel," said Mark. "If your father and half of the CIA gave up trying to understand these ... UCTs ... well, what hope would I have figuring them out with my meager resources, even if I've seen them up close and personal?"

"Wait a minute—"

He pounded the table, knocking the photos around. "Let me finish! Ricky died taking these pictures. Now somebody is ready to commit burglary and even murder to make them disappear. This 'somebody' must know more than we do. *That changes everything.* I want to find these people and talk to them. I want to make them spit out the truth! In God's name, I demand to know what they know! I owe it to Ricky."

I couldn't tell if he was trembling because of our near-crash among the tree trunks or because he'd gotten so angry he could barely hold his fork.

"Do you want to know what I think?" I asked.

He raised his eyes from the prints to me.

"In the world of Intelligence you'll find everything: geniuses and crooks, some honest people loyal to the country and also some low-lifes who'd sell their mother and father and slit your throat for thirty bucks."

"So what?"

"I've never worked for these guys, but I've seen them, lurking in the shadows of high tech. They're all around us. It's not hard to spot them. I think I understand how they function. These aren't people you call on the phone to say, 'I want to register a complaint about one of your drivers who narrowly missed my ass with his convertible'!"

Mark gave a reluctant smile, but he retorted, "It must be possible to track them to their lair. Any organization, no matter how secret, needs external contacts in order to exist. It must have a balance sheet, assets and liabilities, suppliers, channels you can track in order to infiltrate them, to force the system to react."

"You think like a good banker. But the people who ransacked Ricky's bedroom and threw 60-foot pine trees across our path— They're not the kind of people who follow the usual rules."

A seagull alighted on top of a post. It watched us with a curious eye. Mark persisted. "The Freedom of Information Act, you know what that is? I have access to the best lawyers in California. We can force the government to open dozens of inquiries, to follow the trail of official documents all the way to Reagan, back to Truman if we have to. We can uncover who gave the orders, who voted the budgets for the secret study!"

I shook my head. "It won't work. They'll have covers and cut-outs. The trail will take you back to your friend, General Crawford and his ilk, with their stories about dirigibles. There are projects that are so secret they escape any investigation. They're called Special Access Programs, or SAPs. That's what drove my father bonkers. They're exempt from any disclosure, immune to the Freedom of Information Act. They're bureaucratically invisible, even if their budget is measured in billions of dollars. The exact term is 'Waived, unacknowledged special access programs'. "

Mark fell silent. He finished eating his omelet. The two fellows aboard the barge started their engine with a puff of blue smoke. My eyes were drawn to the horizon where the first rays of the sun were breaking up into horizontal streaks. I marvelled at the spots of light they cast over the top of the masts. It seemed like all the boats in the harbor were exchanging signals. The seagull took advantage of this quiet moment to dive towards Mark's plate and fly away, its wide wings brushing us, carrying a stolen sausage in its beak.

I knew the signs: when he was thinking intently and nearing a mental breakthrough, Mark always turned somber and very calm, the exact opposite of his normal behavior. I did not interfere with his concentration, waiting for him to come out of his reverie.

"I know what we need to do. Reverse the process! Take the whole system backward. Like a retrovirus."

He'd spoken so softly that I asked him to repeat it.

"We must create a stratagem. I'm going to assume you're right—"

"Thanks a lot for your trust! It's about time—"

"But even so, that super-secret organization of yours isn't so secret after all."

"I don't follow you."

"Listen carefully." He showed me his right hand, raised his thumb.

"Data item Number One: *We know it exists.* Secret or not. Because of the burglary."

"Right. And the convertible. Thus far, your logic is flawless."

Mark glared at me. "Don't you see? That's half of the battle right there, knowing it exists. It's not completely secret if it needs to manifest in the outside world."

His hand still in the air, he raised his index finger:

"Data item number two: *We also know it has a specific objective.* It is not open-ended. It exists in order to fulfill a precise mission. Therefore, its agents are vulnerable."

The seagull had finished swallowing the sausage. It was looking at us in a way that reminded me disagreeably of Hitchcocks' horror film, *The Birds.*

Mark made a gesture to shoo it off, with no effect whatsoever.

"Vulnerable or not, we won't find them so easily," I pointed out.

"We don't need to. They'll come to us. You know how to catch a tiger? You tie a goat to a stick, you hide nearby...."

79

"You'd use yourself as bait for a bunch of thugs who just tried to kill us? Men who must be looking for us even now, wanting to finish the job? That's a fine idea, your Stratagem!"

"Wait! That's not what I'm planning. There is one more thing we know about them."

He extended another finger, unfazed by my outburst:

"Data item number three: *They don't have the answer yet.*"

"How do you know that?"

"If they had the truth about these phenomena, they wouldn't be reduced to terrorizing poor slobs like us to steal a few pictures. They wouldn't have to make up stupid stories about dirigibles, or tell lies under oath to Senator Healdsburg."

The whole genius of Mark resided in that last observation. Many researchers had come to the same conclusion as my father, that there must be a super-secret, all-powerful project somewhere; but none had considered the possibility that this all-powerful project didn't know the answer, and was thrashing about randomly, trying to understand the phenomenon.

"What conclusion do you draw from that?"

"I believe we can catch that tiger. All we need to do is to provide what it's looking for."

I saw the waitress walking toward us at a rapid pace.

"Tony just went through a police checkpoint on the road. They asked about you. They wanted to know if he'd seen you or your car. Two guys in suits with official-looking badges are combing the area along with the cops. If I were you, I wouldn't stay here."

I folded the map and rolled up the prints.

"We'll pay for the food…"

"No time for that! Do you see that barge over there? It's about to leave for Creighton's Landing, 20 minutes away, to deliver beer and some new nets. They can take you along and help you disappear. Around here, people stick together.

80

They don't like intruders. The cops won't find your car; it's hidden under a tarp."

I caught her eye—such a vibrant green—and asked, "Aren't we intruders?" My tone was light, but she gave a serious reply softened by a smile.

"Tony vouched for you, that's good enough for us." She hurried us on our way.

The sun was rising above the haze that blanketed the bay. I shivered. As we walked away I could still see the waitress standing on the pier. I'd forgotten to ask her name. The seagull was posturing, victorious, casting a hungry eye towards our unfinished breakfasts.

8

Mark lost no time jumping on board. I handed the prints and my cane over to him, and he held me by the arm as I stepped over the railing. The two men in the barge didn't ask us any questions. The propeller spun faster and faster, the engine humming.

"The name's Kevin. Kevin Ralston," said the younger one, extending his hand. He appeared to be less than thirty years old. "I'm ... Let's just say I'm on vacation here."

"You lost your job, admit it!" said the man at the wheel. He was in his fifties, with a graying beard and a sailor's cap.

"A journalist, anyway, that's always more or less on vacation. Hey, you'd better stay on the look-out for snags."

At low tide, Banderas Bay was dangerous, less than two feet deep in many places, with barely visible reefs. Unless your boat was a kayak, you had to carefully decipher the smallest eddy. Every summer, tourists were found frozen and hungry, their motorboats stuck in the mud and reeds of an undetected swamp, waiting for the tide to lift them out again.

It was still too early for us to encounter any fishermen. Ahead of us was the vast expanse of the bay; to the left of the barge we could see Banderas Point, a 15-mile-long narrow peninsula shaped like a sleeping crocodile. It was a protected wilderness reserve of the State of California. To our right the landscape encompassed a row of hills, some clumps of trees, a few houses overlooking sandy beaches. Our boat made slow progress. I took advantage of the quiet time to start a conversation with Kevin, asking about his origins, and his previous work in journalism.

"My folks come from Joplin, Missouri," he answered, "near the Oklahoma border. I did some international reporting and a few articles on technology for the local paper. After that I got an offer from the *Business Times*, in Silicon Valley. When the Internet bubble burst, I ended up on the street."

Mark's head wound had started bleeding again. The man with the cap noticed it.

"You ought to take care of that," he said. "I know someone at Creighton's Landing who can look at it."

He turned to his companion. "Take them to see Dolly. Tell her to find them a place to stay for a few days."

He looked us up and down. "These two need a little rest!"

"All right, Colonel," answered the young man.

"Colonel?" I said. "I thought you were a sailor…"

"The name's Steve Lewis. Kevin and I, we met in Bosnia. Uncle Sam had shipped me there with a dozen tanks. Kevin was doing a story for his paper."

Mark's cell phone rang — Beethoven again. He pulled it from his pocket and stared at the screen. He had subscribed to an automated service that relayed stock market information. A series of figures were rolling by, share prices of a dozen companies at the starting bell in New York. A message followed.

"They're postponing our initial public offering for a month," read Mark. "George must be furious."

"Not to mention Goldenstar!"

"If I were you, I'd get rid of this gadget," said Lewis, looking at the cell phone disapprovingly. "Unless you want everybody to know where you are. Cell phones are as easy to spot as a flare."

By himself, Mark would never have parted with his digital assistant, which served as his phone, computer, scheduling system and message handler. When I extended my hand, he reluctantly turned it over. I yanked out the battery and threw the thing away as far as I could, back towards the harbor we were leaving behind. I felt liberated when it vanished with a splash.

The land occupied by Creighton's Landing extended over a couple of miles along Banderas Bay and twice as far in the direction of the hills. Old man Creighton had settled on the coast in pioneer days and left the property to his two sons. A third generation was managing it now. Curiously, they had not succumbed to the irresistible lure of real estate speculation. While they could have built an entire town next to the water, they preferred keeping their open land, half as camping grounds and half as a small craft harbor. As we approached from the bay side we could see a wooden jetty for Sunday fishermen and a row of motor homes parked under the trees.

Kevin jumped out of the barge as soon as it touched the pier. The colonel threw a line to him. We followed the young journalist along a path bordered by wild grass that snaked among ramshackle cabins, boats on trailers, and tiny cottages.

Further away, along a well-maintained pasture, vacationers with proper reservations could connect their heavy trailers to electrical hook-ups. A dozen cows with calves grazed there. The clever Creighton family was leasing out the same land twice, to tourists and to small ranchers. The sun put a festive appearance on a scene that could have resembled a third-world shantytown. Squeezed close together, trailers and mobile homes improvised randomly-drawn streets. Dogs trotted among vehicles long past their glory days on the open road, now stranded here, propped up on cinder blocks. Improvised stairs led to the thresholds of their front doors. Emblazoned on their flanks — made of aluminum or plastic, and dented by the insults of time — were enchanting or adventurous names:

84

Southwind, Explorer, Wanderer. Others found their inspiration in Indian legends, with mythical tribal names like *Winnebago* or *Apache*.

A few owners had extended their cottages with terraces made of boards nailed together. We passed a very official-looking white and red sign marking a single parking space:

RESERVED FOR EMPLOYEE OF THE MONTH.

I showed it to Mark:

"This one isn't about to head back to the office."

"That's for Kramer's van," remarked Kevin. "And this is Dolly's place."

It looked like a submarine with its rounded bow and improvised tower, evidently soldered onto the roof by an enthusiastic sheet-iron craftsman. A sailor's statue stood in front, carved out of a tree trunk. He greeted us, wearing a blazer, smoking his pipe, grinning under his cap. A white picket fence bordered the wooden steps, amidst a profusion of roses and climbing nasturtiums. On the roof a parabolic dish was aimed at a point on the celestial equator. Seagulls whirled around without bothering the sparrows that were picking at crumbs on the gravel path.

A garden with tomatoes, some grapes, green bushes and sunflowers filled all the space between this metal dwelling and its neighbor. We could hear a TV. A woman was laughing inside.

"Dolly! We need you!" called out Kevin, pulling on the string attached to a bell.

She stepped onto the threshold, a cup of coffee in her hand. Beyond the open door I could see a young couple sitting on a sofa, watching a car race on television. Dolly was a black woman in her fifties. She had the happy, cheerful demeanor of those nurses who make you feel better the moment they step into your hospital room. Before we could say anything, she spotted Mark's bleeding and took control. Five minutes later the TV was off and Mark

85

was stretched out on the sofa under a bright lamp while Dolly, armed with tweezers and cotton dipped in alcohol, examined his wound.

"No wonder it's bleeding; you've got glass shards all over your scalp!" she said. "That won't heal all by itself!"

As she tended to Mark, she questioned us. Where were we lodging? Did we plan to stay some time? Colonel Lewis rejoined us and explained in a few words that we needed to find a quiet retreat. Watching their smiles, I had the feeling that local folks were used to this kind of situation. They offered us a large rectangular mobile home some distance from the others, at the foot of the dunes. Its owner was away in Hawaii for a few weeks. For a handful of dollars he rented the two-bedroom vehicle, a battered aluminum Starcraft made in Detroit in the sixties.

Mark Harris, the well-known investment banker, accepted the offer with gratitude.

We were only two hours away by car from Silicon Valley, with its laboratories and luxurious buildings, but our new surroundings resembled a refugee camp. Susan had left me because, as she said, our artificial universe was lacking in normal people and humanity. What would she say if she were to see us now, exhausted, hurt, in our wrinkled clothes, begging the hospitality of a group of drifters in a place that didn't appear on any map?

But it wasn't Susan I dreamed about when I lay down, utterly worn-out, on the folding bed that was the only piece of furniture in the bedroom of the Starcraft.

Plunging into the canyon, the road kept sinking under my steps, turning into a torrent lit up with moonlight glows. It cut deep and deeper still under a cathedral of black rocks that stood vertically like organ pipes made of basalt. Slower, a moving sidewalk picked me up. I could feel it vibrating under my feet while I ran through the darkness. Monstrous sculptures revealed themselves to my left and right amidst electrical lightning spit out by hidden machines. Pieces of equipment were lining up. They slowed down to a smooth gliding motion, the light much softer now, as if we were entering a museum.

Mark stood on a balcony next to my father. They gestured at me, Mark holding a silver disk. I couldn't remember what I wanted to tell them. The moving sidewalk swept me away.

When I came out on the opposite side of the building, night had fallen and the sky was clear. The stars were very bright. A light detached itself from the zenith, sparkling like a Christmas tree ornament. It came down in a spiral, passed above me with a rush of air that threw me down against the hard metal. When I raised my head again, a woman was looking at me, a young woman with green eyes: the waitress from Mary's café. Her mocking laughter stung me. As I stared at her, she transformed herself, undoing her hair into a blonde aura. Her legs stretched out, her arms ballooned; she multiplied herself. Such vibrant light emanated from her that my eyes flew open.

Colonel Lewis and Kevin Ralston were standing on the threshold of the motor home. Behind them I could see the pasture drowning in sunshine.

"What time is it?" I asked, stunned.

"Four in the afternoon. We brought you a few things."

The journalist put a plastic bag down on the small table next to my bed. He pulled from it toothbrushes, toothpaste, two razors, a few T-shirts, and sneakers for Mark and me, to replace our city shoes.

Mark had heard us. He came out of the second bedroom, rubbing his eyes. Lewis sat down on the edge of my bed.

"Suppose you told us what's bringing us the pleasure of your company? Perhaps we could help you guys."

Mark and I looked at each other. What did we have to lose, if we took them into our confidence? After the attack on the road, it was hard to think of anything worse. Mark went over to a high shelf and picked up the printouts. He unrolled them over the green carpet of the motor home with as much aplomb as a casino dealer spreading out a deck of cards. Then it was the colonel's turn to start rubbing his eyes.

<u>9</u>

Late that afternoon, Kevin Ralston, Colonel Lewis, Dolly, and Tony Kramer joined Mark and me. Lewis suggested we meet behind his mobile home, away from the cluster of caravans. There, everyone listened to our tale. The story fascinated them for different reasons.

Lewis had parked his metal monster close to a water hookup and an electric post, which afforded him a certain level of comfort. Next to it, he had built a wooden shack to shelter his motorcycle and keep a few supplies. He had rigged up a fence around his little camp to cut down on the wind and to discourage wandering cows from intruding into his domain. He pulled half a dozen folding chairs from his storage shed and fixed us coffee.

I was beginning to feel more secure. My physical and mental balance, shaken by the night's events, was returning to normal. Mark, too, was recovering his calm among this little group. He hardly seemed to miss his digital assistant.

Kevin's only neighbors were 200 feet away. A retired couple, they lived in a huge Winnebago equipped with a satellite dish and two poles bearing the American flag and the Jolly Roger.

Dolly told us about watching an unknown object when she lived with her parents in Louisiana. Their car had come upon a luminous disk which had taken off at incredible speed, leaving a circular imprint in a field. Many people had seen the craft. The sheriff had come over the next day to take pictures of the traces, but he had refused to write an official report.

Kevin, displaying a young man's passion for unusual experiences, was taking plenty of notes. Kramer had never seen anything strange in the sky, but he had served in the Air Force on a base located in Thule, Greenland. After their tours on watch and aided by a few rounds of beer, radar technicians shared troubling remarks about super-fast objects that flew at the edge of the atmosphere and played with the jets secretly vectored to intercept them.

Lewis listened in silence to all of this. He was the last to speak, which he did after unrolling and carefully inspecting the images from Brazil.

"I never saw anything like that in the army," he began. "But I've heard stories – some so bizarre I decided I'd best spend the rest of my days on my boat, fishing for salmon and keeping my head down."

He sipped some coffee as if to gather up his courage, and then set his cup down.

"I started out in accounting and auditing – as a civilian, understand. I was too young for Vietnam. Later, when I did enlist, they sent me to Somalia, and after that Yugoslavia. In between I served in the Pentagon – the Defense Department – in financial services. Twice I got involved in internal audits of classified projects, part of the Black Budget. We were supposed to track down significant sums for which the Secretary couldn't identify the appropriations authority. In both instances, I traced it to groups of experts working on the UFO problem, and both times they had no intention of telling us anything about their business."

In the same movement, all of us had put down our glasses and cups, our attention riveted on Lewis. The man was tense, as if reliving a frightening ordeal.

"It all started with a routine request from high up: Congress was talking budget cuts. For the military – no matter what country – that's a bigger crisis than war. We were ordered to account for all research and development projects, including the classified ones. About twenty of us did the work, under exceptional security procedures. And

90

the money didn't balance. The four-star general running the project told us to try harder. So we did. And that's when we stumbled on a project that didn't fit into any category. The project managers told our boss they were studying extraterrestrial material and that it was none of our damn business. End of investigation. But a few years later it happened again; another one of the top brass was tasked with an audit so we ran the same course, with the same result."

"What year was this?" inquired Mark.

"The second audit took place about 1995. The first one, a few years before, I don't remember the exact date."

"How much money was missing?"

This question also came from Mark, which reassured me about his mental state: his financial reflexes were clearly back.

Lewis answered calmly, "Several billion dollars."

Kevin gave a soft whistle.

"Not easy to hide," commented Kramer.

"Easier than you'd think, when it's a secret item hidden among classified projects, none of which are accountable to anybody you know."

"Did you get to the bottom of it?"

"Not really. My chief called the experts on the carpet. They stayed very cool. He grew furious, demanded to know what the fuck was going on. I saw it all; I was there. He asked if it had to do with new weapons, spying, surveillance, special ops, counter-espionage, nuclear material, biodefense, Russian devices, Chinese missiles. Each time the answer was no. Finally they told him flat out that he had no jurisdiction over their project, and they didn't owe him any information. I thought he'd blow his top. Their legal counsel advised them to tell the truth. That's when they said they were analyzing unidentified flying objects, with limited success. Hundreds of scientists had been cleared for the project, from every discipline. That seemed curious to me."

91

"And it remains a secret?" asked Kevin. "I thought nobody could keep a secret for very long in Washington. Look at Iran-Contra, Watergate – "

"You're mistaken. The security budget was five times higher than the technical research money. The security around the project was obscene. That's the exact term my chief used: obscene. And they didn't show him anything, in the end."

"He didn't move heaven and earth to find out more?"

"Well, he tried. He went straight up the chain of command – until advised that if he kept on asking questions, he'd lose two stars. That got him thinking -- especially when a journalist from the *Boston Globe* mentioned the whole business in print. His buddies had a field day. So he gave up, and I decided to go fishing."

The air had turned cool, and the sun was setting behind the dunes. Above our neighbor's camp, the pirate flag flapped. Strains of country music drifted to us: "*You picked a fine time to leave me, Lucille…*"

"It's not that I don't believe you," said Mark, "but what does this prove? You never got into their inner circle; you never saw the Holy of Holies. Suppose they got a physical trace of some object, or even material samples from it, and they can't interpret it. They can't put it to use. We have no way of knowing. Or – they may have fed you a cover story. All of this could have to do with something else entirely."

Lewis pointed at the pictures. "That's why these photographs are so valuable. They provide proof that these craft do exist!"

"Do you think this secret project you stumbled on is still active?"

"No doubt! I also think they have some critical data. It would have to be stupefying in order to warrant this level of secrecy. But our two audits must have scared them. I think they've transferred the project outside of the government – into private industry."

"Why would they ever do that?" asked Kevin. "They'd run the risk of losing control."

"Just the opposite! In private hands, the project isn't subject to any official audit. They can split it up, divide it among a few companies trusted by the Pentagon. People who keep their own secrets. You'll never find them. A Lockheed, a TRW, for instance. They're exempt from freedom of information rules. The Act doesn't touch them. That's why I feel so frustrated, like everybody else who's brushed up against this thing, who know something really big is being kept under wraps."

"We'll just have to force the tiger out of his lair," said Mark calmly.

The others looked at him in surprise. I pushed him along: "Go ahead, Mark. Tell them your idea."

Mark spelled out his three conclusions. Steve Lewis had made clear the secret project was unlikely to have arrived at a scientific explanation. The time had come to bring the truth out. For now, at least, that was our dream.

The homeless black woman had wrapped herself in an old blanket. In front of her, on the sidewalk, was a nearly empty bottle of red wine and a metal box with a dollar bill and a few coins. She crouched in the doorstep of a shop, like so many poor people on the streets of San Francisco who still waited for the mayor's humanitarian plans to become reality.

John Brannan had just left his car in the garage. He was walking home at a steady pace.

"A little coin, Gov'nor!" begged the woman.
John was used to it; there were five thousand homeless people like her in the whole city.

"So I can buy something to eat..."

He couldn't hold back a smile when he saw the bottle. Yet the woman's eyes weren't those of an old drunk. She seemed alert, even wistful. She was challenging him.

"... or buy myself a computer... "

John couldn't resist asking, "What would you do with a computer?"

"I'd invent new electronic circuits; circuits with a low absorption coefficient."

John had written his dissertation about such circuits. He froze in amazement. The beggar got up, still wrapped in her blanket. She pulled him by the arm, making sure no one could overhear them. She left the bottle behind.

"We need to talk seriously, Dr. Brannan."

"You know my name? What do you want to talk about?"

"Your friend, Mark Harris. If you can keep quiet about it."

"You know where Mark is?"

"He wants to see you."

"Can you prove it? "

She pulled out a note from Mark, with his signature. She motioned him to follow. Just around the corner, Kevin was waiting behind the wheel of a car. He drove them to Creighton's Landing.

When John saw Mark's wound and Dolly's bandages, he recoiled in fear, an academic confronted with raw, unexpected reality. I showed him the large-size prints of Ricky's photos. He asked me a volley of technical questions. I had to explain every step of the image processing job my father had done. He wanted to know where my father had worked, on what NASA projects, and the specs for his current computer. It was a regular interrogation, like an oral exam for the doctorate.

In the end Brannan was inclined to accept the reality -- whatever its nature -- behind the photographs.

"I've never believed in those things," he said as if to apologize.

Kramer pulled another folding chair from his shack, adding it to our circle in the pasture. John sat down heavily. A brasero warmed us, shining random spots of light on our faces. I imagined us as cowboys hunkered down around a campfire after a long day on the range. The neighbor's stereo flooded us with oldies.

"When the two of you got back from Brazil," said John, "I did believe you'd seen something. But I chalked it up to the Brazilian military experimenting with some kind of underwater missile. With or without the Pentagon's knowledge."

Lewis put the pictures under his nose again :

"John, I've served in the U.S. Army for over twenty years. No missile, even an underwater missile, looks anything like these."

"Still, to say these are something more.... People have been reporting UFOs for half a century, and nothing's ever come of it. Their existence has never been verified experimentally."

"There's some compelling evidence," said Dolly. "All the major TV stations have talked about it. There's even been some serious journalism, like Peter Jennings, God rest his soul."

"I've seen the stuff," John said derisively. "Some video documentaries about a spaceship crashing at Roswell, and the autopsy of the so-called pilot, a dwarf with a big head. Don't tell me you believe that junk! Come on! Some anonymous cameraman discovers after 40 years that he's recorded the event of the century? And he refuses to release the original film so an expert can examine it?"

"Yes, I do believe it," stated Dolly. "That rancher in Roswell discovered fragments of an unknown metal. The military confiscated every piece of it. A couple years ago, a colonel wrote a book saying he had seen some bodies at the crash site."

"Are you saying Mark's son died because of extraterrestrials?" asked Brannan.

"We're not saying that! Who's talking about extraterrestrials?" Mark protested.

"Any phenomenon that leaves no evidence cannot be verified. Roswell is a series of interesting stories with no proof. Human testimony – "

"How do you know it didn't leave any evidence?" Lewis broke in. He went on to tell John the story he'd told us about his chief, lost in the maze of a cryptocracy whose level of secrecy, to those who had scrutinized it, was obscene.

"There must be some proof, but those who keep it have no incentive to reveal it, especially if they don't have the whole answer," observed Mark. "Lies are mixed in with some elements of reality. If we want to know the truth we'll have to go and extract it the hard way, John. That's why I need your help."

Brannan pulled out some paper and started taking notes. A whitish moon rose over Banderas Bay. The neighbors turned off their CD player and went to bed. In the growing chill of night, we squeezed closer to the brasero while Mark went on sketching out his plan.

It was an incongruous place for a course in physics. Mark had been thinking about the new Nanotronics chip. He said there might be a way to put its stealth mode to good use.

"What does this have to do with your stories about unknown objects?" John asked.

"Stay with me just a minute longer. The burglary and the attack on the road prove there's a group out there, desperate to find out what these craft are, with all the power and money of an industrial organization behind them. They must want it badly, if they're ready to kill for it. I propose to give them what they're looking for. We'll manufacture it: a genuine fake UFO!"

"The goat to bait the tiger," added Lewis.

John eyed us skeptically. Mark pressed on:

"Here's what I propose. We find an isolated spot where our very own flying saucer can land. We make sure it gets wide publicity, including the fact that witnesses have picked up physical samples."

96

"Then…what?"

"We wait for the tiger to come sniffing around."

"That's not too hard," mused John, who was getting caught up in the plan. "A few cameras, well-placed…"

"…as long as we can follow these guys closely and track them to their lair after they pick up the bait – the artifact you're about to make for them," added Mark.

"Me?" asked John.

"Yes, you and Linda Levinson, if you think we can count on her discretion…."

John was warming up to the idea. "I can come back with her tomorrow."

"Too dangerous," said Lewis. "We took a chance when we sent Dolly into town. There must be lots of people looking for Mark and Robert now."

John Brannan could only confirm it.

"George Preston just hired Pinkerton Investigative Services. They're combing the Bay Area and expanding their search to all of California. The FBI came to the office today. They stayed in his office behind closed doors for two hours. And the managers of Goldenstar are calling every morning, asking if you've been found."

"You see! We have to move fast. Tell me more about the stealth mode."

"If somebody wanted to broadcast a signal without being detected by current methods, that would be the ideal way to do it."

Now John was in his favorite domain. He was one of those scientists who could give a lecture anywhere; all he needed was an audience willing to listen. Whether standing at a lectern at Stanford, dressed in black robes and a mortarboard, or sitting in some California pasture, attended by the cows we could hear blowing on the other side of our fabric fence, John was happy to display his technical knowledge. The only thing missing was a white board for him to draw diagrams and charts.

"What we've demonstrated wasn't feasible prior to the invention of quantum detection systems," he began. "You've heard of Maxwell's Equations, of course? They define the basis of electromagnetism. You learn that in college. Well, it turns out some of the theoretical solutions are actually independent of the presence of a magnetic or electric field, but they've never been developed."

I had to interrupt his lecture. "I'm already lost, John. You just said that Maxwell defines electromagnetism."

He didn't get annoyed, he simply started again in a slower, almost conciliatory tone:

"Very few people know that these solutions exist. Instead of using the field components, you work only with the scalar and vector potentials."

"Why don't you just tell us about the practical implications," suggested Mark, who seemed as lost as I was.

"They are extraordinary!" continued Brannan, bursting with enthusiasm. "To begin with, there's no possibility of shielding, since transmission doesn't induce any current or charge in the conductor as it propagates."

"Do you mean to say this is a mode of communication without attenuation?"

"No attenuation, and no detection using a classic antenna, since the electromagnetic field is nil. The signal goes over a much greater distance, too. It doesn't follow the inverse square law! Its intensity goes down as a factor of distance, not the square of distance. You could send a message across the Earth to someone in Australia like they were one town over. I'll tell you, I'm thinking Nobel Prize."

"If we survive," I muttered.

Mark brushed aside both John's enthusiasm and my gloom. "So, how do we detect it ourselves?"

"We'll use a quantum interference detector, of the Josephson junction type. I'll give the design to Linda. She can work on it this weekend, when there's almost no one in the lab. Nobody will ask any questions."

98

"How long will it take?" asked Kevin, clearly fascinated by the idea.

"One week, perhaps less," answered Brannan. "Once you figure out the principle, building the equipment isn't hard."

"It will take us that long to find a good site and set the trap," said Lewis.

He wasn't talking about fishing any more. I sensed that he was ready to pick up the challenge of a new campaign, one where he could coordinate the maneuvers. His reflexes as a soldier were resurfacing.

"Do you have some spot in mind for your operation?" he asked. "Perhaps we should land the saucer in the desert?"

"Too open," I said. "We need to stay on the spot so we can monitor who comes and goes, who is nosing around asking questions, but we also need to remain hidden."

"Especially after we disclose that there's a physical sample," added Kevin.

Mark had the last word. "What we need is a small, isolated town. Two streets, one gas station, one small church painted white, one drugstore at the corner, and a police station with three cops."

Kevin drove John back to San Francisco in Kramer's pick-up. We put out the brasero, folded the chairs, and I went to bed.

It took me a long time to fall asleep. I wasn't thinking about Mark, or the stealth mode, or the events in Brazil. In spite of myself, a hundred questions came to mind about the girl with the green eyes: what was she doing right now? Where was she? Did she remember us? I had thought of a plan to see her again but the whole region must be under surveillance, and I might place her in danger if I tried to contact her. It was a risk I could not justify to myself.

At night, at Creighton's Landing, no sound came to trouble one's rest except from the waves gliding up the shore. I did fall asleep, and it was the sun that woke me up; the sun, and the smell of coffee that Mark was preparing in the trailer's kitchenette. We were like tourists on vacation. That idea made me smile when I took out the new sandals Lewis had bought for us and slipped them on my feet.

<u>10</u>

Later in the day, Kevin picked John up in the city and brought him to Creighton's Landing, demonstrating once again, to judge by John's white face, the same facility in avoiding tails. John came up the walk clutching his briefcase, which was filled with documents to be signed.

"Did you go to the bank?" asked Mark.

John gave him a look of admiration tinged with envy.

"Your name opens every door in the Valley! It must be nice to have a rep like that. I went to Silicon Valley Trust, where a VP just gushed about how pleased he was to be of service to you, Mark Harris, especially when I added that we were counting on his bank for total discretion until we finish our research. I think he had a flashback to the bubble days. I put my name in as secretary, to get things started. You sign here, on this line, as president. I put Robert in as vice-president. We now have an account open with them, under the name of Signal Engineering, Inc."

Seeing how we looked at each other in puzzlement, he added, "I picked the first name that came into my head."

"What about the attorneys?"

"They didn't ask any questions," John said. "They're incorporating us in Nevada and sending an agent to Carson City to expedite it. We'll be officially in business by Tuesday. I gave my home as the mailing address."

"They didn't ask where I was?"

"I told them you were launching a new startup – a big deal that had to remain secret – and that you'd be back at Nanotronics in a few days. They'll be quiet. They're bound by lawyer-client confidentiality. Besides, they know which side their bread is buttered on."

John pulled out a page covered with regulatory statements and bank stamps.

"You need to sign this to sell the shares held in your Lazard Frères account and wire the funds to Silicon Valley Trust. Two million dollars, as you instructed. That'll be effective next week. In the meantime, I've advanced ten thousand dollars from my own account. They'll start printing checks."

They hadn't asked me to contribute to the startup fund. I didn't enjoy Mark's wealth, or even Brannan's resources. My divorce had been a financial disaster. For Mark Harris, this was routine. He had started dozens of companies, along with his associates. Banks knew him and trusted his signature. There was no need for a lengthy investigation to find out if he would honor his commitments. If he requested a little discretion for a few months, that was fine too, well within the practices of high technology investors.

Mark and I signed the incorporation documents, but I still harbored a lingering doubt.

"There's a risk that Mark's accounts are being watched."

"We'll have to take that chance," Mark answered calmly. "From now on we should pay cash for as many expenses as possible, or use our friends' credit cards, and reimburse them as we go."

"The risk isn't imminent," broke in John. "It'll take time for the transaction to be recorded and passed into corporate-level accounting, so we have a few weeks. By then, either the stratagem will have worked, or...."

"Or what?"

"We'll never know what happened in Brazil," said John, "or where the craft came from when they sank your boat."

Silently, I completed the thought: "We'll never know why Ricky died."

There was a knock at the trailer's door. Kramer was still wearing his T-shirt with the beer company logo and his Yankees baseball cap.

"Come over and meet with the Colonel. Kevin has an idea for the site."

We followed him to his camp among the cows. It was Friday night; tourists were arriving in convoys. We saw SUVs loaded with kids, open trucks carrying tents and inflatable boats, and heavy vehicles that went up the slope huffing and puffing.

It was hard to recognize the place where we had met just the evening before. Newly-arrived campers halted at the entrance cabin, paid ten bucks per car for one night on a camping site, more for a trailer. Some of them bought firewood, ice for their cocktails. They settled in the pasture at random, wherever there was space available. Those who arrived first took shelter next to the dunes; they only had a couple hundred feet or so to get to the water. Others preferred the side of the hills, where kids could play volley-ball or launch their kites while their parents set up camp.

We found Kevin in deep discussion with the Colonel, poring over a roadmap they had spread on a folding table. The young journalist had drawn a circle around a specific place.

"It's a little town in Oklahoma, one hour east of Tulsa," he said, pointing at a road, a red wavy line that snaked towards Missouri. "It's just across the state line from Joplin, where my family lives."

Route 44 came from Oklahoma City, went through Tulsa and on towards the northeast, in the direction of Springfield, Missouri. It ran tangent to the circle Kevin had drawn.

"The place is too small to show up on this map," Kevin went on. "It's called Corrals. When I started reporting on the local news, I made a friend there. He was starting a local paper called the *Daily Observer*. If I understand Mark's idea, this would be the perfect spot: accessible but not too much, culturally stuck fifty years behind the rest of

America. You can get to know all the key people in one afternoon."

"Does your friend still live there?" I asked, looking closely at the map. Corrals was at the intersection of four states: Oklahoma, Missouri, Kansas and Arkansas.

"I can get his phone number," Kevin answered. "His name's Allen Lucas. I haven't seen him in two years, but that's not a region where people move around very much."

The operator located the *Daily Observer*, and Kevin engaged in an animated discussion with a secretary there. It seemed the paper had prospered. By the time his friend had hung up ten minutes later, Kevin had promised to write him a human interest piece about the tribulations of an innocent country boy caught up in the hell of Silicon Valley.

We quickly agreed on a plan: Mark and the Colonel would make an assessment of Corrals. Kevin would establish a local base there and plan a beachhead suitable for our group. We trusted Kevin. He had demonstrated his resourcefulness.

Two big trucks drove up near Kramer's trailer, pulling vehicles that looked more like prefab houses than motor homes. They parked them at right angles to each other, and then they parked the trucks to form the other two sides of the square, as if they expected to be attacked by angry Sioux Indians during the night.

Two families came out of the trucks: first, the kids with their backpacks filled with multicolored plastic toys, then the mothers wearing shorts and tank tops, rushing to spread inflatable mattresses, barbecue sets and kitchen accessories. They loaded groceries into polystyrene chests they'd filled with ice bought at the entrance. The men set up the trailers, deployed TV antennas and satellite dishes, and raised their favorite flags to the tops of poles: the Stars and Stripes came first, followed by the pennant of a football team and the red and black flag of the Confederacy. The latter was forbidden in Georgia because it reminded people of slavery days, and this taboo aspect made it the new symbol of revolt among people who disliked political correctness.

A thunderous din engulfed the proceedings as half a dozen Harleys rolled in. The riders parked their hogs close to the new camp and shouted greetings back and forth, with much slapping of backs and dirty jokes. Beer was flowing by the time Kevin said he was ready to go, his backpack loaded with supplies for the trip to Corrals.

We walked with him to the harbor landing, where he had left his car. The path took us past a hangar that served as a repair shop for banged-up canoes and engines in need of a tune-up. A tall, bearded man was greasing a pulley-block. A steel cable hung from the top of the structure. Two brand new kayaks rested on sawhorses. In one corner, two employees wearing big glasses and masks were polishing a fiberglass surface, rounded to form the hull of a fishing boat.

Lewis stopped in his tracks. "Do you ever build boats on special order?" he asked.

"Depends on size," answered the bearded guy. "We're not equipped to compete with a real builder. But if you've got some plans, bring them over; we'll see what we can do."

Lewis pointed at the boat that was taking shape under the buffing wheels:

"A hull of this type, some 12 feet long, how much would it weigh?"

"A hundred pounds, maybe more."

"Could you build a half-sphere?"

The bearded fellow evidently thought Lewis was making fun of him. "That's not a boat, a half sphere!"

"It's for an industrial display," answered Mark. "Not really a boat to go on the water. Rather a disk, with a dome. Kind of a flying saucer shape."

The prospect of manufacturing such a device didn't seem to bother the man. He kept a professional attitude, raising a grease-stained hand to indicate the row of large colored sheets stacked up in wooden cases along a wall of his shop.

"I'd need to know more. The exact size and shape, how strong it needs to be, hull thickness, weight issues. I can't tell you just like that."

"I'll talk it over with my friends," said Lewis. "I'll come back with the layout. How long do you figure it would take?"

"About ten days. We're very busy."

"If we pay extra, can you rush the job? Do it in a week?" asked Mark.

"We'll just have to see."

The man didn't want to commit, but we could feel he was ready to negotiate.

"The project is coming along," I thought while walking back to the Starcraft. "Another push to perfect some details of our expedition, and we'll have our extraterrestrial vessel…."

As for the American town where it would land, I would just have to trust Kevin.

About two o'clock in the morning I woke suddenly, thinking I'd heard a commotion in the tiny kitchen area of the StarCraft. I found Mark there, opening a can of soda. His eyes were red; he looked terrible.

"Another nightmare. I have them every night." He sighed, looking apologetic. "I see those craft all over again, the wave that engulfed us. And I see my son."

What could I say? I opened the fridge and pulled out another can. We sat in the front of the vehicle, on either side of the Formica tabletop.

I hadn't slept very well myself. I felt discouraged after reading several books I had collected about the UFO phenomenon. I shared my impressions with Mark, to get his mind on other topics.

"No useful information in all that," I said in summary. "Most of the writers mean well, but they have a personal

106

agenda. They select the cases they find convenient, even if they have to bend what the witnesses are saying. You find visionaries, conspiracy theorists, false prophets. The worst of the bunch are the skeptics, who view themselves as rationalists -- though they've never bothered going into the field. The charlatans are bad enough, but they pale in comparison to the pontificating academics -- who think they're protecting us from magical thinking."

"When the scientific establishment forgets its role is to serve the public, it turns into one huge hypocritical enterprise," Mark observed. "Do you recall that little company we financed five years ago? The founders claimed they could offer broadband over noisy copper lines. All the experts said it was impossible, without even looking at the data. A good thing we never listened to them!"

I showed him the pile of books Kevin had collected for me, the product of his excursions among used bookstores in little coastal towns: cheap paperbacks, disfigured by angry readers' comments, passages underlined in red, torn pages. The message was all the more eloquent: a large, if marginal audience fed on this type of literature. People were looking for answers.

"When it comes to UFOs, scientists are sneeringly insincere, even the most recognized authorities. From your local astronomer to the Academy of Sciences, they try to get rid of the problem by heaping ridicule on the witnesses. Then there's the media, interested only in its entertainment value, from extraterrestrial autopsies to abduction by reptoids, and even testimony by fake secret agents filmed in the dark, who claim to have brushed elbows with horrible humanoids in underground bases...."

"Fake documentaries always sell better than factual reports," said Mark. "Every journalist knows that."

"The subject is shrouded in so many lies and myths that a secret group could indeed remain undetected for a long time, as Lewis claims."

107

"It's up to us to detect them," concluded Mark, stifling a yawn. "Thanks, buddy, I feel better after talking about this stuff. Even if we haven't solved the puzzle. Let's try to sleep on all this, and have some good ideas for tomorrow."

When John Brannan came back to Creighton's Landing on Sunday morning, he had trouble finding our StarCraft in the middle of all the tents. Our hamlet had turned into a town of four or five thousand people, covered with antennas and parabolic dishes, exploding with gaily waving flags and fluttering kites. Campfire smoke blended with that of a hundred barbecues. The smell of grilled meat permeated the landscape.

John brought us two items: a sealed, egg-shaped device the size of a football, and a black box containing an electronic circuit, a light display and a dial with a simple arrow. The red light of a diode was blinking steadily.

"Linda understood what was involved right away. She's done a terrific job. She spent the night on it. It's pretty crude, but you can detect the signal a hundred miles away." Proudly holding up the silver football, he added, "I've been working on the transmitter myself."

The device was ovoid in shape and made of metal, with a highly polished surface that cast iridescent reflections. It wouldn't take much to imagine it had fallen off a flying saucer. Mark's smile left no doubt. He picked it up and hefted it, as if to convince himself it was hermetically sealed.

"The circuit is embedded in the mass of the material," added John. "If you move the transmitter, look how easily I can track you!"

He changed a setting inside the black box and the needle followed Mark, who had picked up the egg-shaped artifact and was walking in ever-widening circles around the motor home. The tension dissipated, and we congratulated John, laughing like kids with a brand new toy.

Our neighbors called us over to share their hot dogs. We brought a few six packs of beer and spent the rest of the afternoon watching the Cowboys beat the Forty-Niners 45 to 14.

Thanks to Linda's work, we were ahead of schedule. It was decided that the next day, a Monday, I would join Kevin in Corrals, to prepare the landing of what Mark was calling our genuine fake UFO and to set the trap.

The plane to Tulsa had taken off on time. I settled in seat 17A and opened a financial magazine. To defeat probable surveillance of passenger lists, I had registered under Lewis'name. He had lent me his driver's license and a credit card, after training me to imitate his signature. Given the overbooked plane, attendants didn't have much time to verify every detail; they simply checked that the name on the boarding pass matched the person's ID. Lewis'picture looked vaguely like me, and he was only older by a few years. I got on board without any problem, a carry-on bag as my only luggage.

The plane reached cruising altitude over the Central Valley. The airline was running on a reduced budget, so it had also reduced the space allocated to passengers in economy class. My leg, stuck between my bag and the bulkhead of the plane, was hurting badly. No lunch on board, either: passengers shared a basket loaded with power bars and cookies. When it arrived at my level I was shocked to realize that the blonde in row 16 who handed me the basket was the waitress from Mary's Café.

Her eyes were sparkling when she turned around and told me, "The ones with peanut butter are the best in the bunch!"

Was she aware I had registered under a false name? How could she have known where I was going? Would she stop in Tulsa, or would she go on to another city, perhaps never to return to California? Troubled, I promised myself I

109

would find her upon disembarking. This time, I would get her name.

She had caught sight of my magazine.

"Do you know of any interesting investments, these days?" She asked over the seat back, her green eyes drilling into mine.

Without thinking, I fired back, "Should I assume you're interested in finance?"

Right away, I regretted answering her question with another question. On a light tone, she ended our conversation. "I've heard that in matters of finance, one should never assume anything." She turned around and left me staring mutely at her seat back.

As we reached the desert west of Los Angeles, we encountered some choppy air. The plane started vibrating. The atmosphere had a bluish tint, a shimmering appearance, shot through with silvery splashes. I felt sick, as if sliding between two watery layers. I was seeing complex structures that combined and reassembled over a stammering music, my head burning, the air like an inferno. The cells of my brain seemed to stretch and join, stretch and join, and I felt on the verge of discovering some sublime truth that would also hurt me.

There was a bump; the plane steadied itself. A soft drink made me feel better. I pretended to go back to my reading, but my heart wasn't in it. When we landed, I found the hallways crowded. The passengers from row 16 were long gone when I emerged, and I found no trace of the beautiful woman who had made fun of me.

Part Three

CORRALS, Oklahoma

11

Kevin had not lied to us: Corrals, Oklahoma, was a small town with two streets, a wooden church painted white, a gas station and a single drugstore. In the car I'd rented in Tulsa, it took me an hour and a half to reach it. I spent the time reliving recent events and agonizing about my future. As I prepared to mount what Mark called his stratagem, I thought about the experiences of my life and became keenly aware of my solitude. This disarray of the soul, the self-pity that catches the occasional traveller in an unknown town, hit me fully when I settled into the lodgings Kevin had arranged in anticipation of my arrival: a simple studio with a kitchenette. It was part of an amateurish construction, an improvised addition above a garage, the sort of place that real estate ads call "charming in-law quarters." It was attached to a main house, a squarish building painted white like the church, with two large windows that overlooked the main square. The whole property belonged to Allen Lucas, the journalist who had offered to shelter Kevin. It served as national headquarters, editorial office and distribution center for the *Daily Observer*.

I put down my bag and looked over the landscape. Suddenly, I had a flash of premonition: I might spend the rest of my life in Corrals. This square with its two streets extended by curving paths bordered with flowers, this wooden church, the city hall building that resembled a miniature copy of the White House, the school a bit further back, the pasture that doubled as a sports stadium, everything suggested such a simple, satisfying lifestyle that further desire seemed superfluous. It is the genius of small country towns to suspend time and sweep away futility. California may brag about Silicon Valley and the miracles of electronics or about Hollywood with the wonders of cinema, but Corrals, Oklahoma, with its 300 souls, reflected a deeper, more genuine America, which didn't seem to have a care in the world.

I felt myself drifting, lost between two worlds: the cleanrooms at Nanotronics, where one could only enter clothed with a kind of plastic diving suit that rendered one faceless, nameless – and this blessed place that seemed torn out of some naive painting, where every living soul knew every other. A poster stapled near the door of the church called parishioners to simple pleasures. It read: BINGO – EVERY TUESDAY NIGHT.

My heart beat more slowly, my brain found a new quiet rhythm as I went on questioning my fate. I had left my colleagues without a trace, travelling under a false identity, all in the crazy hope of solving a mystery so tough that generations of investigators had broken their backs on it. What reality was I denying, carried away by a deceptive high-tech rush to an invisible, unreachable horizon? Why was I hiding here, far from my familiar environment? Was it from myself I was running, rather than from alleged agents of some black project, or the hypothetical beings of the Amazon? Was it because of this flaw in my character that Susan had left me? I didn't even have room in my heart for my own father, whose only crime was his failure, in my eyes, to fight the bureaucracy of science....

Kevin came over to pick me up at dinner time. He brought Allen Lucas, a big fellow wearing a black turtleneck sweater and a leather jacket.

"Happy to be part of the team!" he said, squeezing my hand.

"I've told him the whole story," said Kevin. "Was that OK?"

"You can't hide anything from a journalist," I joked to make them feel at ease.

Allen took us to the balcony. From there, we could see all the way to the end of the town, where Shockley Street led to the expressway. On the other side the fields and the farms were beginning to fade away in the evening haze.

"There you have it!" said Kevin with an obvious sense of achievement. "Corrals, Oklahoma. The ideal place for the landing of a spaceship. First Contact with our space brothers. A turning point for Humanity!"

The house was strategically located. An alley behind the garage would allow us to come and go without being noticed by passersby on the square.

"Where do you plan to set up the webcams?"

He pointed to the expressway. "The first one, over there, aimed at the turn. It'll pick up the license plates of arriving cars as they take the exit. The second one right here, to survey the square and the church. I'll show you the other sites on the map."

"What about Internet access?"

Allen pretended to be shocked. "You take us for country bumpkins? The cable follows the main road, with a spur down this way. The *Observer*'s been wired for broadband since last year."

I made appreciative noises, and Allen beamed. "Let's go have dinner! You're my guests."

We climbed into the *Daily Observer*'s official vehicle – an old station wagon – and headed out of town, because Corrals presented few culinary opportunities. Allen knew a truckstop less than ten miles away on the road to Joplin with a restaurant, Lori's Place, that seemed straight out of the fifties, with red vinyl seats, linoleum floor and aluminum counter. The music was just as old, but it

114

produced the right level of noise to cover our conversation. Seated by a window, Allen pointed beyond the parking lot: across the way was a rectangular, two-story motel, ten rooms on each level. A convenient, if unsophisticated shelter.

"The rest of the team could stay here," he suggested, "rather than settling in town, where strangers stand out like a sore thumb. The motel has Internet access, too; no need to use cellphones."

We ordered fried chicken and hamburgers and went over the steps of the plan, feeling like conspirators or burglars about to rob some bank. Some key information was still lacking.

"The idea is to make an unusual flying object appear in front of independent witnesses, ordinary people going about their daily business," I said to set the stage. "For them to be credible, we have to give them time to react and even to photograph the craft."

"This'll happen at night?" asked Kevin.

"At sunset. The craft will be lit up. It will have laser beams that sweep the ground. It will touch down to make an imprint, then take off quickly, leaving an artifact behind. Physical evidence! We'll need someone on the spot to pick it up."

"That's the hook, then. What happens after that?"

"Your paper will publish the story. You know what I mean: Witnesses are interviewed. They confirm everything. The person who picked up the evidence is located, but refuses to give it away. More pictures. The story will make the news around the world."

"And what happens after that?" Allen asked again, visibly delighted at the notion of publishing such a story.

"After that? We just wait. All we need is a place where the rest of the team can settle without attracting notice."

"I have a suggestion," said Kevin. He unfolded the latest issue of the *Daily Observer* and pointed to the Classifieds section. He ran his finger down one column.

115

"Here it is. A house for sale, near the Southland drugstore. You can see it from our office. There's a front door facing the street but the garage is only visible from the fields; we can access it discreetly, and keep an eye on it from here with a single webcam."

"How much for that house?"

"It belongs to a widow, Mrs. Applegate. She plans to go join her sister in Florida. The property is on the market for $150,000."

The picture didn't show much detail, but we could put the big garage to good use. I also scanned the job offers, thinking about Dolly. She would be our perfect witness to pick up the evidence and keep it hidden. A prominently-displayed ad caught my attention: the county's Social Services department was looking for reliable people who could assist the elderly. Everything seemed to click: Dolly was trained as a nurse.

We ordered coffee and apple pie for everyone, and then it was time for me to set up my laptop and send my first report from the field to Colonel Lewis.

The next morning, as I got out of bed and looked out, I noticed the crane. How could I have missed it? It towered over the landscape. Every day we pass by telegraph poles, power lines, transformers, industrial equipment we don't pay attention to because we're carried along by our own thoughts and worries or the song we happen to be hearing on the radio. The crane dwarfed the buildings in the town. Twice as high as the church steeple, at least.

"They've started building an overpass on the expressway," said Allen when I asked him about it.

"Can you make some inquiries? Find out the name of the company?"

"Tell us your idea. What do you plan to do with a crane?"

"Borrow it." I grinned at them. "I merely wish to hang our saucer from it and swing the thing around. That will make its motion more credible. The perfect landing would be in three stages. First, observation of an object above the town. Second, it gets bigger, flies over the rooftops and lands in the square, right over there, crushing a few bushes. Then before anybody can touch it—"

"They'll be much too scared!" Kevin broke in with a laugh.

"Still, we ought to plan for it. So it has to take off right away, straight up into the sky, leaving the artifact behind, the metal evidence, with our transmitter inside. Phase three: the object recedes, becoming a simple sphere in the sky, flying off to infinity."

"Cranes don't move to infinity," Allen pointed out.

"We'll hide the disk after it moves back up beyond the square, replace it with a balloon launched at the right moment; witnesses will make the link. They'll perceive it as a continuous trajectory; it's a classic illusion. On the video – obviously, there'll be a video – you'll think you see a single object, lost among the stars."

They greeted my plan enthusiastically.

"When do we start?" asked Kevin.

I answered with as much authority as I could muster, as if everything was in place. "We'll gather up the whole team, with Lewis and Brannan. That will take a week. They'll drive over here in a truck, carrying the device under a tarp. That should give Dolly time to meet up with us and get a job in Corrals. We'll need Kramer, too, to drive the crane."

"There'll be a lot of work for the *Daily Observer*," observed Allen. "We've got to draft a press release to be sent around the morning after; we'll have to interview the witnesses...."

"Don't worry," broke in Kevin, pointing to the square where people had started going about their business. It was filling up with strollers and townspeople on errands. "You'll have a front-row seat!"

All day, we ran experiments with the cameras, equipped with wireless systems that demanded thorough tests of their transmitters. In the evening, gathered in the editorial room of the *Daily Observer*, we checked that we could observe the major places in the town. All of our webcams performed flawlessly. We could read the license plate of any car that left the expressway.

As the sun was about to set, we noticed the bingo players, about thirty people converging on the church. In spite of the gathering dusk, details of their movements were clear on our screens. Most of them were of retirement age. There were elderly ladies in small groups, a few couples. I turned to Allen, motioning toward the screen that displayed a camera's eye view of the church grounds:

"Meet our witnesses! Serious folks who go to church services regularly. They're past the age of making up silly stories as a joke. Our craft will land right in front of them, next Tuesday."

The week passed so quickly that I didn't have much time to think about the consequences of our actions in case something went wrong. We were skirting the edges of the law. What would happen if one of the innocent witnesses, overcome with emotion at the sight of our craft, died of a heart attack? What would we do if our artifact, our so-called extraterrestrial evidence, misfunctioned or fell into the hands of some group that turned out to be of no interest? Those were risks we had to take, all the time refining our plans to minimize the chance of such a mishap.

Dolly arrived on Thursday. The job with Social Services was still open. She had a successful interview, on the strength of her professional record, and was assigned the position of live-in aide for an old woman who lived alone and was dangerously absent-minded. Dolly would shop for her, prepare meals, keep the house in order. She would have her own bedroom.

Tony Kramer rejoined our team by the evening flight. He registered at the motel. We had dinner with him at Lori's

Place before taking him around the town. He looked up at the crane with a big smile.

"I haven't worked with one of those for years," he said, "but cranes are like bicycles; some skills you never forget!"

"This baby is owned by an enterprise from Joplin – Missouri Earthworks," said Allen. "At the moment the project is behind schedule, so they're not recruiting, but you could put in an application just in case. Especially if you tell them you're flexible, salary-wise."

The evening brought word from Mark over the Internet: our device was built and delivered. The Signal Engineering Company, Inc., had officially taken possession of a genuine fiberglass saucer. They were loading it on a truck. Lewis and Mark would start driving at dawn, taking turns at the wheel. John would fly in the next day. He would rent a car in Tulsa and sleep at the motel. He was designing a special system to light up the disk from inside.

I slept quite well that night, for the first time since I'd arrived in Corrals. My mind was at peace now. California was a far-away memory. I had given up on reading books that claimed to explain the UFO phenomenon. In weeks to come, were we not about to delve into everything that could possibly be learned regarding the mystery? I savored this happy delusion as I drifted to sleep above Allen Lucas' garage while Corrals sank into the blue night of Oklahoma.

12

The red, white and blue movers' truck arrived on Friday morning, right on schedule, to pick up Mrs. Applegate's furniture. The real estate agent who supervised the operation, a little fellow with a jaunty mustache, assured Allen that the *Daily Observer* could occupy the house the very next day. The happy news that the paper was expanding had gotten around the town. In a hurry to collect his commission and delighted with such a quick sale, the man had asked no questions. Allen had made it known he would take the property "as is" and would pay for any repairs. The locals did not need to know that he'd be financed by Signal Engineering, Inc.

Over our webcams, we watched as the widow Applegate drove her Cadillac out of the garage, cast one last look at her house and took the road to Florida without undue regrets at leaving Oklahoma behind. We had not haggled about price or conditions. She must have made a very nice profit on an old structure she had been sharing for years with an army of termites.

On Saturday Allen Lucas drove to Joplin with Tony, under the pretext of interviewing the managers of Missouri Earthworks, the company that was building the overpass near Corrals. He had already taken pictures of the work area and drafted a bit of reporting for them to review. Pleased with such free publicity, the owners invited them to lunch. In the course of the conversation they learned that Kramer was familiar with their equipment, the crane in particular. They already had someone, but the man was busy driving bulldozers at another site. Kramer was offered a test for Monday.

There was little more we could do until Mark and the Colonel joined us. An email message told us they had just driven around Albuquerque and were approaching the northern part of Texas.

Sunday was spent setting up computer equipment inside Mrs. Applegate's house and getting the rooms ready for our friends. The old lady had not bothered to clean up the garage, where trash had accumulated for a quarter century. We found a collection of *National Geographic* magazines, tennis rackets that must not have been used since Miss Applegate was in college, and boxes of postcards, memories of journeys to various idyllic locations. We also discovered a treasure: a forgotten bottle of old rum, probably a gift. Did it come from an aspiring boyfriend, hoping he'd be invited to enter the house, to sit by the fireplace, to sip a few glasses? Or was it set aside by the deceased husband, a good bottle left to age in a corner of the garage and eventually forgotten? Kevin entertained us with his fanciful theories about the romantic life of the former owner, in spite of the lack of any clues among the items she had left behind on dusty shelves.

John Brannan arrived in town with a big suitcase, loaded with diagrams and blueprints. He commandeered the second floor and turned it into a workshop. We had barely finished sweeping the garage when Mark and Lewis arrived in the truck. On the flat bed, hidden by a green tarp, rested the UFO. It was menacing, smooth, mysterious, stuffed with special effects. John wanted to do the fine tuning on the spot. He was anxious to see the crane, to make sure our preparations would be sheltered from observation behind the fences surrounding the construction site, and to review the calibration of the cameras: he expressed doubts about the clarity of nighttime details. He had installed a number of small lasers around the circumference of the disk. They were radio-controlled and would emit impressive beams, harmless for an observer. But every action programmed into the saucer was set in a particular sequence as a function of the site, as John explained to us with multiple equations. Allen took him to see the church, the bushes on the square, and the distance to the crane that rose so far above the scene that one forgot it was even there.

"Some kid could still look up and see the beam as it swings over," said Kevin. "We need to take attention away from it."

"Or we need to obscure the crane," I pointed out.

"We'll mount a small fog machine on top of the disk," John decided. "Just enough to reinforce the illusion, dissipating a small cloud."

"Who'll take care of the balloon?" asked Mark.

It would be equipped with a small explosive, no more powerful than a firecracker, answered Mark. We would blow it up at the end of the display, when it was safely away from the scene. Kevin would be charged with that operation. Allen would film the events on the square. Mark and I would track the comings and goings of cars in Corrals after the show.

Before leaving California, John had secured the confidential services of a private investigation firm that conducted background checks on personnel entrusted with management responsibilities. They had access to police records and car registration files. In real time, they gave us data on every vehicle that came to Corrals. For the last couple of days I had been sending them license plate numbers through the Internet, so that we already had a baseline on frequent visitors, suppliers and companies with business in town.

When economic activity picked up on Monday, we were able to catalogue our neighbors' normal activities: deliveries to the grocery store and the drugstore, comings and goings of the mayor, the newspaper truck, the mail vans. A doctor came from Tulsa to see a patient, twice in the same day. A State inspector visited the work site where Tony was maneuvering the crane, to the satisfaction of the contractors. A flowershop from Joplin made a delivery of several small trees to a retired couple who owned a garden plot at the edge of the town.

About 2 P.M., while Mark and John were in the garage setting up the gas tanks that would inflate the balloon, we had a moment of panic when a highway patrol car sped into the square. The colonel set up the alert when the black and white appeared on our screens. In spite of our discretion, our activities in such a small town might have awakened some suspicion. Fortunately, it turned out the police were there for a mundane reason: consenting to a teacher's request, the officer had come to speak about his work before a civic education class. The car drove away at the break, and the town resumed its routine.

We spent the evening drafting various releases that the *Daily Observer* would publish soon after the event to accompany pictures and the first 'spontaneous' interviews of the witnesses.

If some intruder had been able to enter Mrs. Applegate's garage on Monday night, he would have found us going over details of the next day's operation, gathered around the device that sat on the flatbed. John had secured the lasers around the periphery. We had tested the controls. Kramer had access to the crane for the day; he had cleared a section of the work area where Kevin would be able to inflate and launch the balloon.

123

We felt like the producers of a media event, gathering the elements of a nighttime show, assigning roles, rehearsing the smallest gesture, anticipating lighting needs and camera placement. As in any show, there were zones of uncertainty that made us nervous. In particular, it was impossible to accurately predict the wind direction. If the balloon blew back towards the town instead of lifting majestically to the stars, our imposture might be unmasked by a sharp observer.

Mark was the most anxious among us. He worried about leaks. Allen Lucas had a girlfriend in Joplin who was beginning to feel neglected. He had used the purchase of the house and the paper's expansion as an excuse to explain his absence to her. It was out of the question to bring her into our plan.

At the same time, we could not stay away from Nanotronics indefinitely. John Brannan would get back on the road to San Francisco the very day after the event, taking with him the device and compromising hardware, but my own absence and especially Mark's would remain unexplained. The *Wall Street Journal* had published an interview with Joost van Vaart, the big boss at Goldenstar, who spoke of potential legal proceedings if the board of directors of Nanotronics did not take immediate, unspecified action. George Preston had intimated that Mark Harris, overwhelmed as he was by the death of his son and tension in his marriage, was temporarily unable to fully assume his responsibilities. General sentiment leaned towards Mark, with an emotional component that could quickly turn to vindictive anger among shareholders and financial analysts if he didn't get back to his office within a reasonable time.

The most delicate operation would be the dropping of the artifact, to be discovered in the bushes by Dolly, in the presence of independent witnesses.

"It's just like Easter eggs," said Colonel Lewis with a laugh. "Parents get up very early to scatter them around, so

124

that the dear little children can search for them with delight in an atmosphere of mystery and amazement. That's how crowds can be manipulated: the public must convince itself that it has found the truth independently, even though it was already waiting, prepared ahead of time. People never know who is really guiding them or misleading them. How many wars could be avoided if people had the good sense to see through all the bags of tricks!"

Kevin burst into laughter. "The economy would collapse!" he said. "And what about the advertising industry? It would vanish overnight. Not to mention the media. We'd be reduced to reprinting boring statements from the Congressional Record...."

"That's not the problem," broke in Mark, tired of these arguments. "Our own Easter egg has to be in place before the object appears, we can't take the chance of dropping it from the disk. At the same time, we run an additional risk that it might be discovered. We don't want some curious kid finding it before the landing."

I suggested that Dolly should be walking around the square just before the event. She could plant the evidence at the proper time. She enjoyed the idea:

"I'll bring the old lady, my patient," she suggested. "I'll tell her the evening air will be good for her. Nobody ever takes notice of a black woman pushing an invalid in a wheelchair!"

All that remained to be done was a final calibration of the signal detector, and filling up the Jeep that John Brannan had rented in Tulsa. We planned to use it to track any intruders bold enough to come and steal the physical evidence we were proffering, the definitive proof of the phenomenon.

"What do you plan to do when this is over?" I asked Kramer.

It was agreed that, on the day after the experiment, he would make an excuse to quit his job as crane operator.

"I'll drive by Los Angeles to see my kids," he answered. "My daughter lives over there. I haven't seen my grandchildren for a year. "

He pulled out their pictures from his wallet, a blonde girl of six or seven years, holding her little brother by the hand.

"What about you? What plans do you have?"

The question shocked me out of my complacency. I hadn't thought about it. I'd assumed I would go back to California with Mark, to help him turn Nanotronics into an industrial success, but suddenly this seemed like a pointless goal, a petty idea.

The weather had changed over the weekend. The wind, the unknown factor that could impact all our plans, had turned: it now came from the north. The air had cooled. Autumn was coming to Oklahoma. Holly was starting to blossom, trees changed their color. Around the town, farmers were getting ready for the next season, readying the fields for the winter wheat crop, planning the next cotton harvest. In the markets we saw bright red tomatoes, full of juice. In private garden plots people were planting cabbages, salads, radishes and potatoes. They complained about locusts and worms.

The webcams showed tractors moving along the roads, along with convoys of cattle trucks. The smell of freshly-cut grass was everywhere, in the dampness of the air. Carried to processing centers, alfalfa would be turned into pellets to feed cattle over the winter.

In the morning, a hundred irrigation systems painted a scene of multiple rainbows, emerging from the ground fog.

I was reminded of natural cycles I never needed to think about as a citizen of a California technopolis that ignored seasons and such common things as snow, ice, temperature extremes, even thunder or hail. In spite of our project's tenuous prospects, something in me felt reassured by the simplicity of this new life, so foreign to mine. What I had taken – and nearly despised – as a country town, turned out to be the center of a vast universe that dwarfed my own categories. In the evening, cattle lined up at the watering troughs. In the morning, heavy trucks from dairy cooperatives criss-crossed the fields along dirt roads.

The earth pulsated according to regular rhythms like a breathing body, sustained by generations of folk with solid beliefs. If the idea of a non-human form of consciousness held such dangerous power, such a great fascination, it was because it collided with this natural cycle and upset an ancestral faith. No wonder people in authority felt it had to be kept hidden, unacknowleged, immune to confession, inadmissible: didn't Colonel Lewis tell us that the radar operators in Greenland had been forbidden to talk about their observations? Our own experiment, the next day, would be a stone thrown into the pond of social conformity. It was designed to attract the attention and the greed of those hidden powers who had assumed the right to keep the public in dismal ignorance.

What right did we have, to drop this stone? All the scientists who had tried to prove the reality of the UFO phenomenon had failed, their arguments rejected under the mocking hypocrisy of their academic colleagues. Allen Hynek, the astronomer who had tried to give respectability to the problem, had been marginalized. Professor James McDonald had committed suicide, disgusted and depressed by the attitude of his peers. Typical of their lack of insight was Frank Drake, the founder of the SETI project that claimed to be seeking signs of extraterrestrial life. As late as 2005 he had stated: "No observation has been recorded in definitive manner; none of the criteria of evidence has been satisfied...." He was speaking of radio signals; yet he had never considered that other data might exist. Like all his skeptical colleagues from Carl Sagan to Donald Menzel, he had never taken the trouble to study any reliable UFO case in the field.

Now the proof existed, contained in Ricky's pictures. We were convinced that others held similar evidence. The craft

127

we had encountered in Brazil were massive, physical objects. We were about to manifest our own evidence, dangled under the very noses of those who made it their business to stifle such marvels. Somebody had described the phenomenon as a control system that followed its own laws. By staging the landing of a "genuine" fake saucer in Corrals, we were about to interfere with that system, introducing a perturbation into its parameters, as John Brannan might say. We had picked this minuscule community as a test site because it was easy to monitor. We also hypothesized that it would be easy to flush any secret project out of the shadows where it had been lurking all these years.

Sorcerer's apprentices? Indeed, and all the way. The events of the Amazon had sealed a relationship between us and an occult force.

Occult: the big word was out.

We were convinced it wasn't the devil that was hiding behind the UFOs, but an infinitely more powerful and dangerous entity. There is something human in Satan's nature and it is the source of his weakness, because the Demiurge had created the angels, as the men, in His own image. The poet Baudelaire called Satan "greatest and most beautiful of the angels," the advisor of seekers, who "knew in which corner of the envious earth the jealous god has hidden the precious stones." Yet we knew the phenomenon we were tracking was stranger than any model imagined by human ideology.

We were about to reveal and then hide the ultimate jewel – an extraterrestrial artifact – hoping that the opinion manipulators, attracted by our insolent trick, would fall into the trap by trying to steal the evidence. This time, we were the tempters. We were challenging both the censors, who were human, and the phenomenon, which wasn't.

Before retiring, we consulted the weather sites on the Internet. Northeast Oklahoma would be sunny the next day. A weak northern wind should carry our balloon far from

Corrals, beyond the expressway, towards an area of scattered ranches where Kevin would go and pick it up under the moist snuffles of cows. We went back to our rooms, leaving the computers on. The screens showed nothing but a sleepy town, serene in its naive normalcy.

13

Tony Kramer's universe held little room for John Brannan's scientific speculations. Even Mark's passion, his quest for answers, left Tony cold. He had come along for the sense of adventure, drawn to a project that dared flaunt conventions and break taboos, much as other men might pursue illicit affairs, patronize strip-tease clubs, join motorcycle gangs or become Internet pirates.

Sitting in the uncomfortable seat of the crane's cabin, Kramer had a perfect view of the town. The last rays of the setting sun cast Corrals into stark relief: the white picket fences bordering gardens, the angle of every roof, the mailboxes lined up at crossroads, the carefully trimmed bushes on either side of cottage doors.

A few locals had lit up a log or two in their fireplaces. Blue smoke rose, tilted by the northern wind. At the foot of his crane, well-hidden between a fence and a prefab hangar, Kramer could see the flatbed covered by a tarp where Brannan and Lewis were busy setting up the orientation devices, the grapnel that would lift the disk, gas cylinders to inflate the balloon and the transformers controlling the power levels of radio transmitters.

Kramer enjoyed the feeling as he recaptured old professional gestures, the touch of a specialist. He loved the feel of the crane's delicate controls under his fingers. He kept within reach a walkie-talkie that Mark had purchased in an Army surplus store. He used it to communicate with the rest of the team, leaving no trace and no phone company bill.

"Heads up! T minus 20," said Steve Lewis in a level voice.

Without engaging the motors, Kramer freed up the pullies of the crane. He monitored the cable as it unwound, stopping it just above the flatbed. Lewis pulled back the tarp, unveiling the craft. Seen from above, the smooth surface of the saucer resembled a white egg, soon to be lit up from inside.

With darkness settling in, the town lights came on. The square, usually deserted in the afternoon, grew animated again. A few people had already gone into the building next to the church, probably to set up the bingo tables. Dolly appeared at the end of Shockley Street, dressed in her white uniform. She was slowly pushing her patient's wheelchair. A canvas bag hung from the handle.

"Attention: T minus 10," came the voice in Kramer's ear.

John Brannan ran the loop of the cable over the crane's hook and gave the thumbs-up sign. With one finger, Kramer increased the tension. The saucer rose from the platform and began swinging freely. He raised it by another few feet. In the square, Dolly and the old lady stopped to admire the central flower bed. The first stars twinkled in the dark sky.

Dolly stepped onto the grass, picked a flower, and, in the same gesture, dropped the artifact into the bushes. She handed the flower to her charge and smiled at a passing couple headed for the church. A small group had assembled at the foot of the steps. Others were arriving.

"Attention: T minus one minute," said Lewis.

The UFO lit up, its surface gaining translucency. Several circular zones came to life. They would be referred to as "portholes" in the next day's gossip. Although Kramer had expected this transfiguration, he was struck by the surreal sight. The fog machine was turned on.

131

At the foot of the crane, Kevin had started inflating the balloon. The western sky had turned to a deep blue, with horizontal bands of purple above the darkened hills.

The voice announced: "Phase One."

For Allen Lucas, who had just emerged from the newspaper office with camera in hand, the spectacle was so striking that he almost missed the precious first moments. A radiant disk was emerging out of the folds of a curious cloud of rolling white vapor. It swung into the violet sky behind the church while a harmonious tone sounded, part humming and part soft whistle. Fascinated, Allen forgot for an instant that the sound was designed to mask the crane's engine and that the object was nothing but a plastic shell. A woman looked up and screamed, jarring Lucas from his reverie. He started filming. Meanwhile, drawn by the alarmed cries of his parishioners, the pastor ran down the steps.

The craft hovered above them now, casting spots of colored light over terrified faces, flowers and bushes. It started moving across the length of the square, appearing about to dash away, but then it returned with a plunging motion.

Dolly pushed her charge out of danger's way even as others ran for cover. As for Allen, he kept filming.

"Phase Two," said the quiet voice, echoing inside the crane's cabin.

The saucer came down to hover just a few feet off the ground; it made a loop and landed, crushing bushes. The sound grew to a shrill vibration; the light from the saucer grew harder and brighter. People shielded their eyes. A few seconds later the craft took off, grazing the pastor's head before rising into the sky and vanishing beyond the trees and the church steeple.

"Phase Three."

In the square, the witnesses were recovering from their initial shock. There were about thirty of them clustered together, eyes intent on the sky where the saucer had receded to a tiny sphere, ascending towards the stars. As it continued to climb, it turned into a fat luminous spot, then just an orange point that dissolved in a flash.

"Careful! It's coming back!" warned an old man who pointed at a yellowish glow on the eastern horizon.

"It's only the Moon rising," said another fellow.

Allen stayed close to the group. He kept shooting, recording live impressions. His camera seized the moment when Dolly noticed a bright object in the bushes, screamed in surprise and lifted the artifact with great care.

"It dropped something!"

"Careful with that! It might be radioactive!" somebody yelled.

Dolly walked up to the camera, holding out the silver egg.

"Do you really think it's dangerous?"

"You ought to put it in a safe place," said Allen with authority. "We'll need to call in some specialists who can analyze it."

Several conversations sprang up. Tension had dropped, along with inhibitions. Everybody wanted to recall the event, comment on it.

"I've always believed in extraterrestrials," said the man who moments before had mistaken the moon for a flying saucer.

"There's got to be life elsewhere...."

Among all the confusion, Dolly and her old patient turned around and headed toward home, taking the artifact with them. Some witnesses had pulled out cell phones to call the police, friends, the Air Force, TV stations. The pastor was deeply troubled. He thought he had seen dark shapes moving around inside the disk. Everybody had forgotten the Bingo game.

Kramer had already swung the beam of the crane over the truck and deposited the disk onto the flatbed. He turned off the engine and climbed down from the cabin. John

133

stretched the tarp over the device. Five minutes had elapsed. While the townspeoples' attention was still fixed on the balloon's last position in the sky, the two of them drove off the worksite, headed for Tulsa, on to Texas, and the road back to California. We had agreed that they would get rid of the compromising object along the way. They would take it apart, dropping unrecognizable components in the public dumps of little towns throughout Death Valley.

A short time later, Kevin took off in the Jeep with Colonel Lewis to recover the balloon's debris. The GPS sensor showed it had crashed in the expected zone, some five miles downwind from Corrals. Once cut into pieces, stuffed into a barrel with some gasoline and burned, no trace of it would survive.

Mark and I had followed the whole operation on webcam screens. We watched the square fill with excited people. Allen moved from one group to another, recording testimonies. As Steve Lewis returned to the house, the first police car was screeching to the spot, siren blaring. People were trampling over the bushes, amazed at the broken branches. Some were tearing out leaves, taking bits of wood as souvenirs.

"The Bingo game has been cancelled," announced the Colonel, rubbing his hands together with glee. "It's a circus down there! The cops saw the object flying above them on the highway—"

"Our balloon…."

"They both saw the flash just before the object disappeared. They swear it was flying against the wind!"

"I'm eager to read all the details in the *Daily Observer*," Mark said, laughing.

I pointed out the time had come to release our first communiqué, drafted the day before. It went out via fax and the Internet, addressed to major press organs, newspapers, TV channels. As soon as Allen came back to the office, we started posting photographs, movie clips, video interviews.

Kevin joined us about 11 P.M., bringing pizzas and beer for our night vigil and some food for the next day, during which we planned to remain hidden while watching developments. He turned on the radio to the local news and listened to the scanner on the police frequency.

Mrs. Applegate's parlor had become the nerve center of our operation. Three TV sets monitored major channels, with the sound turned off, surrounding us with confusing images: a car race in Italy, a riot in Africa, whales playing in Alaskan waters. Mark and I took turns writing down the license plate numbers of cars, and checking them against our baseline list. For the moment, most of the activity on the roads came from the police. About midnight the county sheriff arrived on site. His men had cordoned off a perimeter around the crushed bushes, using yellow ribbon as if for a crime scene. He interrogated the pastor. Two policemen remained on guard, taking down witnesses' names.

At about 2 A.M. the first mention of Corrals appeared on the radio. It was on a nationally-syndicated program, very popular with truckers, insomniacs and night owls across the country. The program gave wide exposure to conspiracy theories, alien abductions, cattle mutilations, and mystical circles in corn fields as well as advertising special gold-plated bracelets and psychics for hire. The host, Mike Ball, was just as comfortable announcing political exposés (when you play recordings of George W. Bush speeches in reverse, you can hear him say "Satan is among us" and "The Martians arrive!") as he was bragging about a new health drink that erased wrinkles from your face.

Mike Ball interrupted his interview with a lady who received nightly visitations from the Archangel Gabriel to break the big news.

"Our Oklahoma correspondents have just told us that a 90-foot UFO landed in the small town of Corrals in front of a crowd of witnesses, crushing all the vegetation in the

135

town square. It happened just a few hours ago, ladies and gentlemen!"

An angry listener immediately called from New York to ask what the Air Force was doing about it. Another reported that the Corrals area had been overflown often by black triangles, and that monster fish had been caught in the neighborhood. This was followed by one minute of advertising for an infrared camera that could record chakra radiations.

"We are now being told that the Corrals UFO left physical traces. A woman, a nurse, saw the craft eject a metallic object."

A listener from Tucson, identifying himself as a ufological expert, called the program to explain that the craft must have been in difficulty due to a lack of magnetism, which had happened before. "The secret archives of the Pentagon are full of cases just like that."

Everybody had forgotten the woman guest of the show. She called herself back to the attention of Mike Ball and the rest of America by stating that the Archangel Gabriel had confided to her, on her pillow, that saucer landings were about to intensify and that The End Times were Nigh. Mike interrupted her to remind his listeners that they could phone the station to order the gold-plated bracelets that would protect them from electrical radiation and might cure certain types of cancer—under medical supervision, naturally.

Secured in the fork of a tree, one of our webcams showed the house where Dolly was now living. Nobody had yet knocked on her door by the time I left for bed about 3 A.M. Mark remained in front of the screens while Kevin and Allen printed their newspaper. Colonel Lewis was already asleep.

I walked through the quiet town on the way to my studio. A police car was still parked next to the crushed bushes. The square was deserted. I thought about John Brannan and

Tony Kramer, who by now should be out of Oklahoma. No trace was left of the balloon. Yet a message survived, imprinted not only on videotape but in the consciousness of witnesses. It would grow to maturity in their dreams. It would be carried over the wordwide web and pass into the collective unconscious, as a Jungian psychologist would have said. It would mix with other elements of belief and myth. The outcome was impossible to predict.

14

Allen Lucas let himself in at seven in the morning and shook me awake. "Get up, Robert! We're in way over our heads," he said, handing me a steaming cup of coffee. "Just look at all these people!"

He pulled back the curtains while I hurriedly started dressing. It was as if the County Fair had begun. The square was filled with media vans parked every which way. Two cops were vainly trying to channel a steady flow of trucks and buses with parabolic dishes on their roofs. Several teams must have arrived early, because they had folding tables and chairs all set up, with big cameras on heavy tripods and black cables snaking through the parking lot. The hum of generators drowned out all other sound.

We ran over to meet with Kevin, who, unshaven and with bloodshot eyes, was busy printing another edition of the newspaper.

"Our distributor in Dallas just asked for a thousand more copies," Kevin said. "We're getting calls from everywhere."

"We're running out of paper," added Allen. "We can't get resupplied before noon. The pictures have gone around the world. We've sold the rights in five countries."

In the team's office at Mrs. Applegate's house, I found the situation just as busy. Without a word, Mark showed me the long list of vehicles he had recorded since dawn. They belonged to local stations as well as big players like CNN and NBC. Then came a flood of curious country folk who had family in Corrals. The sheriff had driven back again, probably more for the opportunity to be seen on TV than for any need to further his investigations.

Mark had welcomed this flood of new people jumping into the thick of the action. It was the release he had been seeking, an antidote for his distress, a feeling that he was at last doing something tangible to answer the loss of his son. But he was clearly exhausted, and I insisted that he take a few hours off and try to sleep.

Colonel Lewis joined me as I was turning up the volume on the TV monitors. We caught a CNN reporter interviewing two experts on extraterrestrial life. A fat yellow-and-red header scrolled across the screen. It read: "Corrals: Invasion or Illusion?"

"These nice folks may well have seen the rising moon," stated Professor Randolph, an astronomer in a three-piece suit, standing in front of a huge picture of the Andromeda galaxy.

"But how does that fit with their testimony that the object rose into the sky and disappeared with a flash?" argued an older man, pensively running his fingers through his gray mustache. He was introduced as the chief investigator for the Consortium of Global Ufological Science, or COGUS.

The astronomer shrugged off the remark. "Simple confusion with a shooting star," he said with authority. "I myself once thought I'd seen a UFO. I was in a plane flying above the Pacific when I saw a moving light. It turned out to be simply a slow meteor, grazing the higher layers of the terrestrial atmosphere."

"Do you plan to conduct a personal investigation of this Oklahoma sighting?" asked the woman reporter.

Randolph seemed shocked at the suggestion.

"Professional scientists hardly have the leisure to investigate everything country folk might perceive as unusual in the sky, Christine. Naturally, should the government request that I go there in an official capacity, I will do my duty as a scientist and as a citizen."

139

"Unfortunately, we're out of time for this fascinating scientific discussion," concluded the reporter. "Stay tuned for further updates during the nine o'clock news."

The next screen was tuned to a religious channel. In contrast to CNN, it had few qualms in stating bold conclusions. A preacher calling himself Father Theo brandished a Bible, while a scrolling banner read, "Corrals: The Eschaton!"

Colonel Lewis turned to me in amazement. "The Eschaton? What the hell is that?"

"I think it has something to do with the Prophecy of the End Times," I told him.

Playing on a screen behind the preacher were color images shot the previous night by Allen Lucas. We could see the disk hovering, oscillating inside a multicolored glow, then majestically moving away.

"Doesn't the Good Book say, in *Revelation* 21:2, '*And I, John, saw the holy city, New Jerusalem, coming down from God out of heaven, prepared as a bride adorned for her husband?*' Is it possible to be any more clear, dear friends? Isn't this marvelous prophecy unfolding before our very eyes?"

The banner at the bottom of the screen was replaced by a phone number as the preacher wiped a tear from his eye and went on.

"The time is approaching when every one of us will have to give an account of our deeds before the Lord. Call us for a prayer, send us your offerings, and stay tuned to this channel to hear the good advice that will guide your conscience!"

By ten o'clock, things had gotten far worse. Our listing of license plates now stretched to several feet, fed by the arrival of curious tourists, fans of the unusual and independent investigators. People converged on Corrals from every corner of America. There were free-lance writers eager to sell a first-hand story to a magazine and wannabe mystics hoping to make a name for themselves in the microcosm of occultism or alternative religion. The pastor had thrown open the doors to the church, which filled with anxious crowds.

A few reporters had gone over to knock on Dolly's door. She had not answered, and her phone was off the hook. A note stuck outside stated, "The person who lives here is not able to receive visitors. Thank you for your consideration."

That didn't stop a few bolder fellows from leaning on the doorbell. A car from the *Tulsa Daily News* was parked by the sidewalk, hoping that Dolly would eventually come out.

"Two more plates just rolled in" announced Lewis, showing the images on the screen. "Both are in the database. They're with GOBUS, based in Los Angeles. Their sworn enemies, OFREP, are already here. Earlier today, they nearly started a fight with the cop who's guarding the bushes we crushed last night."

"What's OFREP?"

"The Organization for Research into Extraterrestrial Phenomena," answered Lewis. "These people hide their ignorance behind convoluted names. They probably believe it impresses the journalists."

The webcam showed a tall young man, loaded with expensive cameras, scanning the grassy area with a Geiger counter while his older colleague took pictures of the town and the church. I recognized the gray-haired man who had been on CNN. They had arrived in a minibus filled with impressive equipment: magnetometers, spectrographs and even a small radar dish, which they eagerly demonstrated in front of curious passersby.

"Let's keep an eye on those," said Lewis, adding, "As if there wasn't enough trouble, Professor Randolph is here too, on a mission for the Air Force, no doubt taking care of public relations."

"They all look pretty harmless to me," said Mark, refreshed after a few hours of sleep. "At least they have the guts to come here and investigate."

141

"I'm not concerned with their ideology," said Lewis. "They can believe whatever they want. I worry about other people, agents who've infiltrated their organization. The group we're looking for would find an ideal cover among these people, precisely because nobody takes them seriously."

"Let's go down there," suggested Mark. "I need some fresh air."

For the folks in Corrals, this particular Wednesday would forever be enshrined in local history. Many families would keep that day's issue of the *Daily Observer* as a treasure to be read again and again and passed on to their children. The landing and its aftermath were as exciting as a circus arriving in town with its monsters and jungle beasts, clowns and trapeze artists in shiny suits. Children ran happily among the television vans. They made a buck or two every time a reporter sent them out to the store to get a pen, a plug, a roll of tape or some other needed item. Grown-ups lined up, hoping to be interviewed. Everyone had an opinion. Small crowds had assembled around the "scientists" of GOBUS and OFREP, who, eyeing one another suspiciously from across the square, began to exchange accusations of charlatanism.

The verbal confrontation was about to turn into a real fight when a truck drove into view with great fanfare. I recognized Father Theo himself at the wheel. He was towing a flatbed with a stage-like construction that reminded me of nineteenth-century Western country fairs. A group of stern disciples in black frocks stood around a display where I was astonished to read, THE RETURN OF THE BEAST and, in smaller characters, THE INVASION OF THE REPTOIDS.

There were about twenty of them. As soon as the truck came to a halt, they jumped down from the platform and fanned out among the crowd, passing out leaflets. "Buy gold. Get ready for the End Times. The Eschaton is

142

marching on!" were some of the headings. Their leader walked toward the church with a firm stride.

In a few hours the humble pastor of Corrals had become something of a celebrity. As a first-hand witness of unimpeachable honesty, he appeared on every channel. In a well-intentioned move, hoping to enlighten his parishioners, he had organized a round table debate in front of his church to discuss the events of the night.

He stood up before the unruly crowd and scratched the microphone.

"Does this work? Can you hear me?" he asked as people in the first few rows covered their ears to shut out the horrible crackling.

"This is not the hour for common technology, my good man," yelled Father Theo. "The time has come to give up such toys, and listen to the Voice of the Lord."

"Everyone will have his turn at the microphone," replied the pastor in a conciliatory tone.

He had not counted on Professor Randolph, who promptly stormed up the church steps, followed by a teen-age boy who cradled a laptop in his arms as if it were a fragile baby.

"As a scientist, I demand a place in this debate," he said. "The Voice of Reason, too, needs to be heard."

"Science is of the Devil," said Father Theo. "Have you no shame?"

The gray-haired chief investigator of GOBUS, who turned out to be named Hubert Tronig, crowded before the mike. He wore a brown jacket with wide lapels, a sky blue tie with red and black flying saucers, and a pin in the shape of an extraterrestrial face with golden almond eyes.

"We have no need of an official astronomer here," he said, facing Randolph. "You'll just insist that the witnesses saw the moon, as if the good people of Corrals couldn't tell our satellite from a spaceship. Everybody knows that the Air

143

Force and the CIA hide the truth. Declassified documents are accumulating within our archives—"

"I've seen them, these archives of yours!" Exclaimed Randolph. "A dozen shoe boxes and a filing cabinet stuffed with newspaper clippings that turned yellow a long time ago!"

"The Lord has revealed to me—" came the voice of Father Theo.

"Please, every speaker in his turn!" Pleaded the pastor.

"Carl Sagan has demonstrated—" Randolph went on.

"Our Visitors—" began Tronig.

"If you don't keep order—"

"Our friends from the Cosmos are coming in peace—"

Gathering himself, Tronig burst through the confusion to grab the mike.

"We are the only true scientists here. I'll tell you what we plan to do. We'll hypnotize the witnesses. You'll see what they tell us: how the extraterrestrials stretched them over a table, gave them medical tests, took bodily fluids from them. This is serious business. What is happening is an infiltration of our society by Aliens. They are polluting our race. Within two generations, the Earth will be populated by their hybrids!"

"Don't listen to such fantasy," warned an older man with white hair who was holding a magnetometer.

A woman went up the steps, raising her hand. "I want to be hypnotized!" she pleaded. "They bother me every night!"

"The Visitors mean well," the old man went on, ignoring the interruption. "They show us the Way of the Cosmos, and the preservation of the environment."

"Why did they crush the bushes, then?" yelled a young cameraman who was clearly enjoying the scene.

"They wanted to point out our mistakes!" replied the ufologist, undeterred.

"What a stupid answer!" interrupted Hubert Tronig. "The Visitors are gathering samples. That's a well-known fact. They study us in the smallest detail—"

"On the contrary," replied the other man. "They already know everything about us. Have you forgotten the Pascagoula case?"

"What about Roswell, then? Huh? What do you make of Roswell?"

"Balderdash!" screamed Randolph. "It was just a balloon!"

"You dare call yourself a scientist. You're just a CIA puppet!"

"Order, please!" cried the pastor, at wit's end.

"We've triggered something, and it's out of our control now," observed Mark, even as a chair sailed over our heads to crash on the sidewalk. The two ufologists were attacking the astronomer.

"We can't undo what's happened," I said. "If you went up to that mike and explained exactly what we've done, nobody would believe you. The Landing at Corrals has become a historical fact. It is truer than truth itself."

Abandoning the church steps where people were busy exchanging blows, Father Theo retreated to his truck, where he armed himself with a megaphone. Part of the crowd followed him, fed up with the chaotic scene around Professor Randolph. The anti-Reptilian disciples had plugged in a tape recorder that played a religious hymn, drowning out the pastor's voice.

Father Theo was starting to explain why the Beast of the Last Days had picked Corrals for its evil manifestation when Mark got a message over his walkie-talkie.

"Dolly's in trouble," he said.

We ran back to the office where Colonel Lewis was waiting.

15

The images on the screen told the story of the attack. In the middle of the riot, two men belonging to Father Theo's group had quietly removed their black coats and blended into the crowd. We could see them walking rapidly towards the old woman's house. A reporter parked out front took notice of them. Our camera caught the ensuing scene. They had pulled him from his car, roughed him up, and jammed a rag over his nose and mouth.

"Chloroform?" asked Mark.

"They threw him back in his car. It'll be at least an hour before he wakes up again."

"Let's go," Colonel Lewis said to me, loading a pistol. "We should be ready for anything. Mark, you better get the Jeep and meet us over there."

"How many of them are there?" I asked, hobbling down the steps, trying to keep up.

"At least four," replied the Colonel. Seeing my cane, he slowed down to let me catch up. "Two big Chevy Blazers were behind the preacher's truck. Their license plates are registered to a mining outfit — something called the Geological Services Company."

"What about the artifact?"

"It's still over there," he answered, showing me the detector, where the signal had not moved.

The intruders had broken a window on the side of the house. When Lewis and I arrived, we found the front door open. Dolly's charge had managed to maneuver her wheelchair onto the front porch. Though she was trying to get someone's attention, everyone who passed was looking towards the square.

"Help me!" she cried to us. "My nurse is hurt!"

We found Dolly in the bathroom, bloody but conscious, applying a bandage to her forehead.

"Don't bother with me," she said. "It's superficial. Go after those guys. They found the artifact." She grimaced. "I guess hiding it behind some books in the library was pretty obvious. They ran off through the back door."

We rushed out through the kitchen, only to get a glimpse of the two Blazers racing towards the expressway, raising dust as they tore across the fields.

"Let's go," said Lewis. "It's our turn to play."

"First, Dolly has to disappear. We need to keep her safe."

"That'll look suspicious. It'll attract attention."

"What's suspicious about wanting to get away after being attacked? It's a natural reaction."

"There's a bus for Tulsa every evening," Dolly told us. "I can take care of myself. I'll leave as soon as I can find a replacement for my patient."

When we came out of the house we found Mark waiting in the Jeep, the engine running. Five minutes later we had left Corrals behind: its picturesque site, its lovely white church, and its population in turmoil. The plan called for Kevin to recover the webcams, wrap up the computer equipment and get ready to drive home. The offices of the *Daily Observer* would return to their old, routine ways. No trace would remain of our team's passage through the town.

At 6 P.M. we left the expressway, still following the two Blazers. The detector showed them three miles ahead, driving towards a semi-desert area near the state border. They seemed to have taken a shortcut. We were moving along a country road bordered on both sides by endless fences. Cows poked their muzzles between strands of barbed wire that marked the boundaries between ranches.

"No need to rush," the colonel said. "What counts is to go on tracking them, without their being aware of us."

An hour later, we passed through the town of Broken Arrow. The landscape beyond grew uncertain as the gathering dusk erased contours. Half an hour later we rejoined Route 44, and in the heart of a tiny hamlet that wasn't even on the map we almost lost track of the Blazers among the confusion of truck convoys headed east. Route 44 became 412 a little later and strayed from Oklahoma and the Kansas state line.

Night had fallen. Our prey was far ahead of us and drove fast, without a stop for gas or food. We only had a small supply in the Jeep, some power bars, mineral water and fruit. We remained silent, caught between the excitement of the chase, the feeling that the experience was headed for its conclusion, and the monotonous hum of the tires on the pavement, the endless night road, the growling of the trucks as we passed them.

Seated behind Lewis, I tried to make sense of the landscape beyond his square shoulders. Other than the illuminated swath of straight road, there was only the occasional flash of a silo or barn wall caught by headlights

Mark kept a stern face, his jaws tense, his eyes scanning the billboards along the way. "Welcome to Arkansas," said a big rectangle lit up by a row of spotlights. A bit further, on the side of a hill, a patriotric group had erected a blue banner with white stars and red lettering, which read, "God Bless America."

From Mark's point of view, our expedition represented a logical development, the culmination of an obsession, his search to fill a vacuum deeper than his life. Nothing, no national secrets, no claims of executive privilege, could stop or even slow down his drive to achieve the impossible.

But what about Colonel Lewis? His commitment grew out of a disappointment with life. After a proud military career, he was put out to pasture. They had thanked him by telling him to get lost in some forsaken place. The future held only old age and a death without glory, without any answers to the questions his life had raised. He had brushed against the enormous evidence of a secret project without being able to ascertain its actual purpose.

One undeniable element remained: the project in question was at the very heart of human destiny, shielded by an unprecedented series of security systems, even more sophisticated than those protecting the Manhattan Project, the development of the atomic bomb. If any doubt had lingered in my mind about the project's reality, it had been erased by their attack at Dolly's house, the stealing of our artifact. The proof of its existence rested in the two Blazers tearing ahead of us through the American landscape at 70 miles an hour.

We followed their agents, flesh-and-blood men who were armed and would not hesitate to fire without warning on ordinary citizens, let alone bothersome intruders like us.

What would we find, at the end of the journey? What were my own motivations as I launched into this venture, with what was left of my life? I must confess to a moment of weakness, a failure of enthusiasm, while the trees blended together under the glow of the headlights and the Jeep tires went on howling.

One could speak of cowardice, in my case. I had been swept along to this spot by my deep friendship with Mark and by what I now recognized as feelings of guilt — not by courage or resolve. Ricky, even as as he was drowning, had glided within my reach. I had touched his hair, just as a wave pulled him away. Even more chilling was the denial that followed. All those who could have told us something — any bit of information about the nature of the tragedy — had lied to us with uncaring arrogance, as if the life of a

149

child did not merit the bending of arbitrary rules made in the name of "national security."

The whole thing was deeply unfair and infuriating, and that was the reason I was in this car, shaking with every hard bump in the road, risking my own life — not Mark's blind passion, nor the need for revenge that motivated Colonel Lewis. What I felt was both more complex and more troubling. There was a sort of detachment in me, mixed with resignation, as if I saw the events from a distance, through a lens. I was fairly certain we would end up dead, but still I kept an atom of logic. Perhaps it was that little detail that saved me, in the end.

I only became aware of this gradually. I had not consciously undertaken this exercise in self-analysis while we were passing cattle trucks and pickups loaded with produce on the expressway that rushed east across the United States.

"Here we go!" Lewis called out, tracking our progress on a map. "We're coming up on an exit. It looks like they're leaving the 412."

The detector signal registered a slow, almost imperceptible deviation. We were too far behind the Blazers to guess at their intentions. Mark took a chance. When we reached Route 62, which cut our own path at a right angle, he turned south, following his intuition. The detector soon confirmed his choice. Now the Jeep was jumping roughly over an uneven road that went through forest, then followed more fences, more ranches. We had been driving for two hours when we reached a place where the Blazers slowed down.

If you could believe the sign posted by the road, Cherokee Flats had four hundred inhabitants. As in Corrals, there was one service station, one general store, and a small cluster of houses. We reached a square devoid of any trees or greenery. Two streets intersected there, with a commercial building at each corner. On one side was a bar with a few motorcycles parked in front. On the opposite side, a mortuary was painted black and white. In the window, decorated with a profusion of plastic flowers, a coffin rested on sawhorses. When we drew abreast of the mortuary, a horrible detail struck me: two white patio chairs had been set up on either side of a round cafe table painted black, supporting an umbrella with alternating black and white sections. The whole setup rested on bright green indoor-outdoor carpeting, as if the undertaker was expecting two ghosts, or was about to offer one last shot of whisky to a recently-deceased customer, to wish him well on the road to eternity.

I shivered at the sight. I grew even more uneasy upon discovering some of the living inhabitants of Cherokee Flats, encountered as we drove along the road that stretched towards the hills. They were ugly, deformed, with pasty whitish faces seemingly carved out of toadstools or puffed up by some fatal mistake of nature. A crippled creature crossed the road in front of us, followed by an obese woman who was little more than a mass of fat. Others dragged themselves along the sidewalks. We recoiled from eyes that glowered at us with lusty greediness, the concupiscence of a squid.

Once we had passed the last few houses, I opened the window to the night's fresh air. Our speed helped chase away these evil sights like a fading nightmare. I concentrated on the landscape. It showed nothing but stones and gravel where I had expected fields, scattered farms, or the welcoming freshness of wooded hills.

The rocks formed a vast plain tinted with purple in the vanishing twilight. The moon was rising in front of us, and this brought my thoughts back to the events of the previous day, to the fallacy of human testimony and to the even greater fallacy of the judgement of experts. We had been swamped by the events our operation had triggered. We had lost control of the images we had released. Now they had a life of their own, floating around in people's minds, uncontrolled, randomly deformed by false inquiries, bizarre beliefs, multiple fantasies. An absurd competition had ensued, where neither the skeptics nor the zealots could guess at the truth. Yet those who called themselves rationalists turned out to be the worst of the bunch. They were not simply twisting the facts, as did many believers; they denied the facts in their totality, in the name of the ideology of reason. Given their preconceived notions, the testimony of the witnesses was not simply wrong, it was impossible. Occam's razor was not used as a neat simplifying tool, but as a castrating instrument.

In my mind, I reviewed the data I had been able to gather from the books Kevin had assembled for me. An illustrious French astronomer, in the sixties, had briefly corresponded with researcher Aimé Michel, who thought he had discovered some geometrical alignments among sightings. The astronomer told Michel, "Your alignments cannot possibly exist, because UFOs cannot possibly exist!"

Another celebrated academic, an American physicist, had stated in the pages of the prestigious *Science Magazine* that the traces left behind by an unknown flying object after a landing could not correspond to an interplanetary spacecraft because no residue of chemical propulsion had been found at the site! And what should we think of the report issued by the University of Colorado? After spending half a million dollars, their committee concluded that the phenomenon was of no interest to science, although fully one third of all the cases they had investigated had resisted all attempts at explanation. That detail had not stopped the American Academy of Sciences from approving the report and burying the UFO question for 30 years, to the considerable relief of the academic community.

The advocates of the reality of the objects deserved credit for recording the testimony of witnesses; but they, too, interpreted it in their own ways. They bent the facts in

152

order to force them into the mold of their preconceived theories. The cycle of absurdity would start again. If the witnesses resisted the process, the believers would hypnotize these poor people again and again, until their tailored statements conformed to the new dogma.

If there were such a thing as a genuine sociology of science, what a rich domain it could find in this completely unexplored field, where the fantasies of zealots merged with the blatant, self-satisfied, officially-sanctioned stupidity of scientists!

Part Four

THE PROJECT

16

"Watch out!" Lewis called, studying the detector display. "They're just ahead of us."

The two Blazers had abruptly slowed down, kicking up a cloud of gray dust. Now they attacked the foothills of a gravel mountain. The signal was very strong. We climbed the slope behind them, no longer attempting to hide. The game was almost over, I thought. The comedy of the two men who had attacked Dolly and stolen the artifact, and the fake disciples of the Eschaton infiltrating the crowd in Corrals — none of that had resisted our analysis. We knew who owned their trucks. Now they would have to answer our questions.

When they got to the top, the Blazers kept going. A short distance behind them, we, in turn, reached the highest point overlooking the landscape. Then I understood our mistake. Stretching as far as the eye could see was a series of whitish mountains looming above dead lakes, polluted ponds, gaping holes and stone structures resembling Mayan ruins, the result of an environmental massacre perpetrated by some large-scale mining operation. There were ruined aqueducts and machine emplacements, enormous traces that seemed a testament to some vanished civilization. The moon was rising over the ghostly scenery. It made the hills seem even more pallid, the betraying shadows more sinister.

The path we followed angled into the gravel slope and stopped before a small shack occupied by men dressed in military garb. A barrier came down before the hood of our

Jeep. A guard carrying a machine gun came toward us. Mark made a U-turn and sped away.

"Did you look at the patch on his uniform?" asked Lewis. "That's absurd, but these guys are Navy! What's the Navy doing among the tailings of an old mine? There isn't any boat here. The closest ocean is hundreds of miles away!"

"The road goes around the facility," said Mark, pointing to a metal fence topped with barbed wire that extended far to the west. "They took our artifact inside."

"It's an old fence," I pointed out. "I'll bet it's down in places."

We saw several patches of light in the hollows between the hills. We speculated that somebody was using the ancient facilities as a training base, or perhaps a research center.

"When I think about the ufologists, looking for the Big Secret in Nevada...Area 51, Nellis Air Force Base...under the open sky.... As if these people had any need of a landing strip! If they've captured a craft, or just some pieces of it, they can do the analysis anywhere! Just look at this — "

We had reached the edge of the dunes, at a point where we could look down on concrete buildings. Armed guards patrolled the lighted perimeter. They all wore Navy uniforms. My father had mentioned that the scientific documents he had studied had been confiscated by the Navy.

"Come to think of it," said Colonel Lewis, "a secret Pentagon project, touching on a topic like this, wouldn't be under the responsibility of a single branch of the military. It would involve the Navy as much as the Army or the Air Force. The tunnels of this mine may be flooded. They could be training divers in there, or testing new weapons."

Mark gave a soft whistle: "A secret group hidden behind a classified project. An enigma wrapped inside a mystery..."

Two miles later we almost got stuck in a swamp. A metallic stench emanated from quiescent water that, in our headlights, glowed with greenish tints.

"Have you noticed?" asked Mark. "No insects. Not a single bird."

We did find a hole in the fence, at a place where the gravel hill had given way under the weight of passing vehicles. There, partly hidden behind a row of small trees and wild brambles, we again spotted the two Blazers as we glided down the slope. They were parked alongside a concrete building. Two parallel walls extended beyond it, forming the entrance to a tunnel. To the right was a watch tower with a spotlight.

Leaving the Jeep under the trees, we ran to the entrance of the old mine. No one challenged us.

"It's a maintenance tunnel," said Lewis, pointing to a row of electrical generators, pumps, metal shelves holding dust-covered tools, all the repair supplies of the old facilities. Several tip-trucks were rusting away on a spur of the rail line.

"Let's go!"

The searchlight swept the bushes behind us, deepening the shadows of the tunnel. We scrambled into the darkness.

Lewis remained close to the maintenance area to guard our backs while Mark and I followed the tracks. We did not meet anyone. Equipped with lights scavanged from the tool shed, we studied the tangle of cables and pipes that dived underground, guiding us.

"They must feel really secure," Mark observed. "No guards inside the tunnel. Only the gate, the barbed wire, the tower with the spotlight...."

"They relaxed the watch when the Blazers came home," I said. "We were just lucky. We'll run into trouble soon enough."

It was another wrong guess. The tracks kept going, ever deeper, with nothing to stop our exploration. Dust drifted down from the roof, the stench of mold and fungus stung our throats, but our path remained clear, without even a surveillance camera to watch us. Though distance was difficult to estimate, we had gone at least half a mile into the tunnel when we felt a rush of fresh air.

"That explains why there's no guards," Mark observed. "This goes nowhere. It ends in an air well to the outside."

"Yet the men from the Blazers came this way," I said. "There's got to be another passage. Let's back up."

We found it as we walked up the slope, halfway to the maintenance area where Lewis waited for us. It was a steel disk — a safety door — sealed into the rock, activated by a simple lever. Again we saw no security precautions, and the door slid aside when I pulled the lever. Mark followed me into a narrow gallery brightly lit by fluorescent tubes. We followed it for what must have been a thousand feet before we came upon technical facilities, probably an old geological and assay laboratory. The place was wide, equipped with white benches, large ventilation hoods, white walls, empty metal cupboards, but no equipment and no trace of any personnel. Fine dust covered everything. At the end of the room a wide slanted window gave a view of another room below, a larger space that may have served, in previous decades, as a repair area for mining equipment, and as a hangar for bulldozers and small trucks, judging by the racks and pumps still bolted to the far wall. The facility was huge, with portals of pharaonic size and heavy columns supporting the rough rock ceiling where some traces of water trickled down.

In the dim light of the hangar we saw a shiny object resting on a work table. It defied description.

At first sight I took it for a section of an aircraft wing. It was curved and looked metallic. Its surface was luminous, with quickly-changing, shimmering glows, as if the mass of the material was radiating. There were men around the table. They seemed intent on several experiments and never looked up, never noticed our presence high up in the wall behind them. Our window must have been just another dark area at the top of the cavern. I kept watching them, concentrating hard on what I saw in spite of a growing migraine that made my head ache and my vision blur.

We heard a bell. The technicians stepped back and looked towards a gallery opening. Several men walked in.

"The guys from the Blazers," said Mark.

They were led by an older man in white overalls with an insignia I did not recognize. They carried our artifact, the physical evidence from Corrals. They placed it next to the shiny metal section, with infinite precautions.

"They seem to expect some reaction," I told Mark.

He stifled a laugh. "They're going to be disappointed!"

They took measurements. They took photographs. They even used an X-ray machine. Next, the scientist in white placed the artifact between the jaws of a vise and sawed it in half with a diamond wheel. The man entrusted one half of the artifact to a young fellow with a crewcut who wore an aviator's leather jacket. He left the other half with the technicians in the room. They were bringing other instruments, getting tests ready.

The shiny wing-like object started palpitating, vacillating like a candle about to die.

My headache was getting worse. It brought tears to my eyes. Mark was not doing well either. He had to grip the edge of the bench to steady himself.

"That's why they don't need any guards," he said in a low voice, forcing every word. "They count on a physiological field to keep people away. Some sort of electromagnetic perimeter."

Perhaps. In any case, the field — or whatever it was — appeared to induce mental confusion, because I thought I saw the shiny object modify its appearance, blur itself into a vanishing glow, then return to its place looking more pointed and wider at the base.

"It changed shape," Mark whispered at my side.

My father, when he had studied Ricky's pictures, had alluded to other dimensions. I hadn't taken him seriously. I couldn't visualize a super-object that compared to to our everyday space and time in the same way that a 3-D object compared to its projection on a flat screen.

My father had also told us that the Pentagon assumed any pilot describing the impossible maneuvers of such objects in the air must be crazy. They would send him to a shrink and he would never again climb into the cockpit of an F-16. Later the unfortunate airman would be assigned to a desk in Alaska, or he would process kerosene supply requests on some god-forsaken base in Minnesota.

I could hardly stay on my feet now. Mark was perspiring heavily; he looked feverish and shaky. The light from the object extended across the window into the room. The men below had stepped back towards the rock walls. They were wearing helmets and special glasses. My brain seemed to shatter.

I was in a garden, or a park where the flowers were endowed with shimmering wings so that they were able to take off and come back, landing again on their stems. They gave off a subtle scent, heavy with Asian references, an absurd mix of jasmine and curry, of incense. A woman arrived. Her feet hardly touched the grass. She smiled at me. It was like lightning, illuminating my life. There was so much tenderness and solicitude in her movements that my mind seemed to expand to the edges of the universe, embracing everything that was alive.

Suddenly, all the flowers vanished. A flame engulfed my vision, blurring my sight. The woman gestured towards me as if to say good-bye. I felt a sharp anticipation of disaster, a sense of great danger.

"Let's get out of here!" I managed to grab Mark by the sleeve. "I don't know what's going on, but the answer isn't here!"

I showed him the technical team, the men in uniform or special suits, still backing away from the shimmering object.

"They don't know any more than we do. Heaven knows where they've found this piece of material, but they're in over their heads...."

Mark still carried the detector. We glanced at the screen. The signal had become a double pointer.

"We'd better follow the guy who's taking the other half away," he said, painfully articulating every syllable as we started to back away from the window. He added, "If I stay here, my head is gonna blow up."

I pulled him away and we back-tracked to the main tunnel, grabbing hold of pipes and the rough edges of the rocks to steady ourselves along the way.

A siren wailed in the distance. We dashed to the maintenance area where Lewis still waited for us.

"Faster!" he yelled, taking each of us by the arm. "Two and a half hours you've been gone! Damn it, you look like corpses."

We didn't have the strength to answer. I would have sworn our exploration in the tunnel had not taken over an hour. He pushed us and pulled us to the Jeep. He threw us inside and took the wheel. The spotlight from the tower fell on us. Men ran out of the concrete building. They started their Blazers. The fellow with the crewcut and the leather jacket was with them.

When they drew close enough they started shooting, with no warning or attempt to block our way. Bullets pierced the back window. As we spun around in the gravel, the Jeep lost traction and stalled. Lewis gave his pistol to Mark. "Cover me," he said, jumping out. He dashed straight at the other vehicle and grabbed the arm of the man holding the rifle. Before the man could adjust his aim, he was rolling in the dust with Lewis on top of him. They struggled for the weapon.

162

Mark started firing at the other car, first aiming at the tires, then the driver when the angle seemed right. The second Blazer, with half of our artifact in it, sped off, disappearing behind a pile of tailings.

Lewis stood up, clutching the rifle. The Blazer was skidding in the dust, all four wheels spinning helplessly. Lewis ran to the front, shattered the side window with the rifle butt, and grabbed for the driver. Gravel flew in a gray blur that obliterated the landscape. The heavy vehicle began sliding down the hill, hesitated at the edge of a ravine, then tumbled over Lewis. It rolled again, once, twice, spilling its contents. It landed on its four wheels again and sped away, out of control, into a green swamp in the hollow between the hills.

When the dust settled, only the roof of the Blazer was visible in the muck. The body of Lewis was stretched out on the hillside. His eyes were open. Blood pooled on his chest.

"Stay with us!" I said, holding his head, crying. "We're gonna make it."

He managed to grin. "Not this time," he whispered.

Mark had jumped down from the Jeep, the pistol still in his hand. He took Lewis' wrist, felt his neck artery, gave me a look of despair. I had to look away when Mark closed his eyes. The crash had scattered everything the Blazer carried: some weapons, a metal box with ammunition, a briefcase full of papers.

The helicopters arrived. They were combat models, the kind you only hear at the last minute as they come swooping down on you. They fired a single salvo from their machine gun. Mark, his pistol useless, dived into a gully. Hidden by the giant cloud of white powder kicked up by the downblast of the rotors, I grabbed the briefcase and crawled to the Jeep. Men glided down from the sky all around Lewis' body. They found Mark and grabbed him by

163

the arms. They took him away and thundered up into the sky in their huge machines.

I was left alone in the Jeep. Of course, it was Mark they wanted. I was a non-entity in their plan; they wouldn't bother with a useless second prisoner. They had won: they owned both halves of what they thought was an alien artifact, and they had Mark, the illustrious financier.

The Jeep started just fine. It slid a little when I switched to four-wheel drive, then it climbed up the hill sideways, like a crab. I got it to crawl in low first gear all the way to a dirt road that led toward Cherokee Flats. The full moon seemed pleased to rise over the inhuman landscape, as if it owned it. On the seat next to me, the detector was intact.

17

When I reached the town, my hands and my knees were shaking so violently that I had to stop the Jeep at the corner of the square. I couldn't have driven any further even if I had been able to see the road through my tears. Leaning on my cane for support, clutching the briefcase as though it was the only thing shielding me from total insanity, I climbed down, lurching and reeling. The door to the bar was open.

It was a cheap honky-tonk without name or grace — just a long formica counter, a narrow space for stools and a few tables in the back. Neon advertisements blinked all over: Coors, Budweiser, Jack Daniels. Several arcade games lined the back wall, offering pinball, video poker, or combat against extraterrestrial invaders. The aliens again. Always the aliens.

The customers were not interplanetary, but they didn't look entirely human either. I settled onto a stool at the bar, briefcase on my lap. To my right was a deformed woman in a flowery dress, her body overflowing the narrow stool. To my left was a young man apparently born with a single eye. The other orbit was obstructed by folds of whitish skin. He tried, horribly, to smile at me. A shot of Stolichnaya slowly settled my nerves.

A tall man came striding through the place, his Stetson pushed to the back of his head. He stopped when he reached my seat.

"You ain't from around here!" There was something child-like in his air of discovery.

"First time visiting Cherokee Flats," I stammered.

"The Arroway mines, you know about that?" He struck the ground with his boot, as if to suggest that the earth was hollow. "It's all Swiss cheese, under there!"

I had to search my memory.

"Arroway? As in Arroway Energy, the electrical batteries?"

"Them's the ones. The whole region, here, it's a hundred square miles of lead mines. Mixed in with nickel, you get the picture?" He winked at me and gave a curt nod in the direction of our neighbors. "They'd never heard of ecology. Fifteen thousand tons of ore processed, at the height of their glory."

"Per month?"

"Per day. The pollution, I won't tell you. That fucking company exported batteries to the world."

I bought him a drink. A seven-and-seven for the cowboy and another vodka for me. For a few minutes I stared in silence at the flytrap ribbons hanging from the ceiling and the blades of the fan that made cigarette smoke swirl. The juke box was screaming an old Roger Miller tune: "*Kansas City Star, that's what I are...*" The woman in the flowery dress attempted a few dance steps. A breeze carried hints of gasoline. The burnt exhaust of motorcycles blended with the bitter smell of beer.

The cowboy put down his drink and looked at me more closely. "Say, you look a bit unsettled. You okay?"

I realized my hands were still shaking. "I got lost," I said.

"That happens," he said pensively, adjusting his hat. He glanced at my cane and my shoes, the briefcase. I pulled it closer and he looked away. "Not too often, but it happens. Folks come from some big city, they ask lots of questions about what's going on down there...." He struck the ground again with his heel, then seemed to study the shadows, as if looking for someone.

"If you want to learn something and not get lost next time, you oughta talk to old Doctor Matt. Over there, by the jukebox."

The man was curled around a glass of bourbon. Judging by the expression on his face, it wasn't his first of the evening.

"Doctor Matt, he may not look it, but he knows an awful lot about what's happened in the holes of the Swiss cheese. Me, I'd rather not ask. I leave it to the folks who come from the big cities."

He looked at me again, quizzically, and added, "At least, in your case, you got out alive." He touched the edge of his Stetson, signaling our conversation was over. "Thanks for the drink," he said politely.

I still felt unsteady. I wouldn't have been able to take the wheel again. I needed to talk to someone. I walked over to the doctor and sat down. The bartender seemed to read my mind, coming over to fill the old man's glass, then mine.

Doctor Matt had a shriveled face that life seemed to have abandoned a long time ago. Add to that a long curved neck and he resembled a vulture. He lifted his head to stare at me. Though his eyes were dulled by whiskey, I detected in them a tiny spark of professional curiosity.

"They send you over here?" he slurred, squinting at the folks at the bar, without a word to thank me for the alcohol. He applied himself to draining the glass.

I glanced about. Nobody was looking at us. The woman still danced. The cowboy was talking to another patron. I extended my hand.

"Nobody sent me, doctor. My name's Robert."

"Usually, folks who come and ask me questions, they're intellectual types, you know what I mean? You — Robert, right? You're not like that. You've been in the mine."

He was the second person to guess it. "How can you tell?"

167

"When a fellow comes in here, unshaved, shoes covered by that fucking white dust, generally, they've seen somethin', right?"

I didn't argue. His reasoning was impeccable, the logic of a drunkard.

"You believe in the Devil, Robert? You think you'll see Hell someday?"

He had spoken loudly, almost a yell, but nobody turned to us, because the juke-box boomed even louder:

> *Out in the West Texas town of El Paso,*
> *I fell in love with a Mexican girl ...*

I hadn't thought about the Devil for a long time. In sunny California under a clear blue sky, with an endless parade of glistening automobiles looping through luxurious hillsides, it was hard to picture Hell. Even the notion of purgatory evoked only some sad, faraway suburb, soft banishment to a boring place. The inhabitants of Pacific Beach, near San Diego, joked about their town. They said the initials, P.B., meant "Paradise on a Budget." Here, in Cherokee Flats, things looked very different.

"What about you, Matt?" I asked. "Do you think demons are after you?"

"Because of the pact," he whispered, staring at the brown liquid in his glass that danced with the reflections of all the neon signs around us. He squeezed the glass as if afraid someone would come and snatch it from him. For a moment I thought he was going crazy, and I wouldn't be able to get anything out of him.

"I don't understand that whole pact business, Matt. You'll have to explain it to me."

He lowered his head. For a moment I thought he'd lost consciousness. But then he started speaking in a low voice, barely audible.

"I was there when they signed the pact. I was born in 1929."

168

He dug into his pocket and pulled out his wallet, then fished about in it, determined to show me his driver's license or some paper to prove his birthdate, but his eyes couldn't focus, and he eventually gave up.

"In 1947 I was 18, old enough for the service. They sent me to New Mexico. I was interested in rockets. I read all the science-fiction stories I could get my hands on. I wanted to take off into space, at the controls of an atomic plane. In June of that year a private pilot saw flying saucers. It was in all the papers."

"Kenneth Arnold," I said, trying to encourage him by displaying my own knowledge.

He stopped cold and drained his glass, then motioned to the bartender for another one.

"Don't interrupt me, Robert, or we'll get nowhere."

He fell into a kind of stupor. I had to shake him to get him started again.

"You were talking about rockets, in New Mexico."

A glint returned to his eyes.

"We used to launch rockets and weather balloons, from White Sands and Roswell. The engineers studied the high atmosphere. They were really into their work. The Nazi scientists, too, the ones who came with von Braun…"

"Project Paperclip?"

"I already told you, don't interrupt! Paperclip was just part of it. People never knew that Uncle Sam had made the same deal with other groups, too. They had their own monster doctors, their own…experiments. It was a game anybody could play."

Matt choked on the last few words. His wrinkled face, sculpted by deep lines, turned ashen — almost a death mask. It took a visible effort for him to go on.

"We had to find out, you see? How could we guess what would happen when humans were sent into space? Radiation… We were barely beginning to understand. When I left the military, I studied medicine. And then I went back to New Mexico to continue experimenting."

169

He halted, as if searching for some revelation buried too deep in his mind, obscured by the fumes of alcohol. He seemed to reach a decision and barked an order.

"Here, give me a hand! I'll show you something. You might as well know the truth."

I helped him from his chair. He leaned heavily on me. Between Matt, the briefcase, and my cane, I was afraid we wouldn't make it, but somehow he managed to lead me outside and down the street. He sagged against the mortuary door and rang the bell repeatedly. A young man finally answered, his hair in disarray, his eyes empty.

"I brought a friend," said Matt. "I'm gonna show him the specimens."

"You think it's a good idea?"

With an effort, Matt stood up very straight.

"My friend is a researcher who comes from the Coast," he said with the blind authority of someone who has had much too much to drink. "He needs to see. He came over just for that."

The fellow put up little resistance as Matt pushed him aside.

He led me through the chapel where clients paid their last respects to the living, through a back office crowded with coffins, arriving at a metal door with a combination lock. Matt stared at the plate with its many keys. He turned to the young man.

"I'm too tired today. You do it!"

"You think it's a good idea?" asked the man again. Like other people I'd seen in town, he seemed affected by what psychologists delicately call an intellectual deficit.

"Since I'm telling you, it's an order!"

Our guide pulled out a piece of paper from his pocket. It bore a series of codes. He worked the tumblers until the lock clicked.

"You're gonna understand what the pact was," said Matt as he pushed open the metal door. The young fellow ran

170

away, leaving us alone in the cold chamber in front of a dozen drawers.

Matt hesitated, selected a drawer, and pulled it open. I saw a glass cylinder resting inside. As the room's cheap fluorescents caught it, I jumped back. The cylinder was filled with a translucent liquid, and floating in it was some sort of being. It was short, perhaps the size of a 10-year old child. It looked human, except for its disproportionately large head. I counted six fingers on each hand. It had no hair whatesoever. As for the eyes, they seemed almost Asian, but were covered by black skin.

Feeling dizzy, I managed to ask, "Is it an extraterrestrial? A real one?"

The doctor didn't bother to answer. He just looked at me as if I was an idiot and shrugged. He spun the cylinder and the little body started tumbling in the liquid. I was about to vomit. Matt's movements now showed greater control, as if the icy chamber had chased away his alcoholic haze, or perhaps he was just recapturing an old professionalism. He closed the drawer with a screeching sound and opened another one, a bit larger. I had to close my eyes and lean against the wall. Matt caught my reaction.

"We can go back now. You've seen what you had to see."

He led me out of the mortuary, down the street, and back at our table in the bar. Feeling weaker than ever, I waited for him to tell me the full story.

"I was their best medical technician. Surgical assistant. I had a good reputation for keeping my mouth shut. I was crazy about space travel, but before we could think about going to the moon we had to understand conditions above the atmosphere. Most of the project scientists thought space radiation — cosmic rays, gamma rays, electrons or protons from the Sun, whatever — would destroy the human body in a hurry. We sent up mice, monkeys, and also human cadavers — short ones like you just saw. We didn't have rockets to put a satellite in orbit, naturally. This was 10

171

years before Sputnik! So we'd hang fancy-looking capsules from special balloons. Meanwhile, on the ground, we built top-secret laboratories where we exposed those poor bastards to radiation."

"Where did you find them?"

"During the war, the enemy experimented on human subjects. Near war's end, our guys captured one of their labs. It wasn't pretty. They would amputate a guy's arm and try to graft it onto someone else. Just to see what would happen. Naturally the death rate was sky high. Most of their subjects had been captured in isolated villages where congenital malformations were pretty common. Like those I just showed you. We took over their patients for our own research."

"That doesn't explain UFOs," I pointed out.

"Wait a minute. The bodies you just saw are human, victims of a thyroid disease called Progeria. We had other patients, in Roswell and White Sands, with Turner's Syndrome and Werner's Syndrome. Our military bosses asked the captured docs to continue their experiments, legal or not. We picked up where they left off. When we heard that the damn Soviets were pushing their biologists to make a homunculus, a diminutive human, for manned space flight experiments, we had to work even harder. From time to time the balloon flights didn't go as well as they should. We ended up with accidents — crashed capsules and little burnt bodies. When people started to talk, we had to cover up with some sort of explanation. That's when we made up the alien story. At the time, Roswell was the world's only air base with nuclear bombers. The Soviets were sniffing all over the place. A flying saucer crash made one helluva diversion."

He drained half of his glass in one gulp.

"So, what does that have to do with real UFOs?" I said again, getting upset.

"There were real UFOs, too. Our guys in White Sands kept filming unknown objects, alongside our rockets. We

172

were never able to intercept them. The technology seemed incredible, and the U.S. wanted it. The top brass in the Pentagon decided to study the phenomenon in secret and to mix it all up so the cotton-picking Russians wouldn't guess at what was really going on. We spread the rumor that the little bodies were extraterrestrial. We got the ufologists to buy into the story. The Pentagon moved the corpses over here."

"What about you, Matt? How did you get to Cherokee Flats?"

"I was cleared for the secret project, at Roswell. I was part of the team that started the cock-and-bull story about a crashed spacecraft. We thought it would help flush out the Soviet moles, by tracking where the story came out again. The radiation tests on Progeria patients, the balloons with the victims we sacrificed, the homunculus project, all that was our pact with the devil. After that, there was all the fallout from the Nuremberg Trials. The U.S. had to stop the experiments or the world would have said we were worse than the Nazis. Naturally, all the technical records were destroyed."

I thought back to our dinner with Stephanie Sheldon at the Senate restaurant. Bennewitz, the physicist, had been fed tall tales about extraterrestrials by government agents. They had made him mad. Literally and deliberately. And when a Senator's assistant had demanded to get the Roswell files for 1947, the Pentagon had told him to go shit in his hat. That all made sense now, in an obscene kind of way. If Matt was telling the truth, the evidence would never, ever, see the light of day.

"What about the secret project, the genuine research about UFOs? Whatever happened to it?"

"When they moved our teams out of New Mexico, they scattered us to four different centers. The main physics studies were transferred here, along with the little bodies to serve as cover for the real research. I was in charge of the transfer."

173

"Why bother? You didn't need these bodies any more."

"The story isn't over. A few years back, we even released a video of an autopsy, pretending we had studied an alien body. Millions of people swallowed the story. The confusion helps in hiding the real stuff. Suppose some nosy Congressman's aide gets wind of the project. We take him in here, we show him the little alien cadavers, and when he's through vomiting all over his expensive suit we tell him to keep his mouth shut and the money coming."

"Why are you telling me all this? I could talk about it—"

"Who'd believe you? You met an old drunk in a bar. I'm nearly 80 years old. There's nothing they can do to me now. I'm on my way to hell anyway."

I made a move to get up, but changed my mind, thinking about the wing-like thing I'd seen in the underground lab.

"I saw something down there," I said. "Something that didn't make a whole lot of sense."

"Oh, you mean that piece of a real saucer. Don't worry about it. Nobody understands it."

I waited, expecting him to laugh. He didn't. "You're telling me it's real?"

"As far as anyone can figure — which isn't much. That project's been going on a long time. Project management's based somewhere else. The guys down here are just a bunch of technicians, space cadets, out of their league. They've been stuck a long time. Even the security's getting lax."

"They must have learned something, over so many years?"

"They watch; they try some experiments, from a distance. As soon as you get close to the damn thing, time starts doing funny stuff to you; it passes at a different rate. People get sick."

I remembered how ill we had gotten down there.

With a disgusted air, he added, "Look around you, the folks in this place. Deformed bodies, stupid minds. That's not just because of the lead mines. People get old faster and

174

faster. Why do you think your beard's grown so much? I knew right away where you'd been. You'd better drop it if you don't want to end up in hell, like me."

This time I got up for good. I was hungry. I abandoned Doctor Matt to his diabolical terrors and convinced the bartender to make me a sandwich. It was almost closing time. Patrons began clearing out. I had started to feel a bit better when the two heavies came in. I recognized their Blazer. They must have figured out there was a detector somewhere, and that Mark didn't have it. A loud explosion just outside set bottles adance. I knew it was my jeep. I left a 50 dollar bill on the counter and made for the men's room. The bartender didn't bother to count out the change. He seemed accustomed to this kind of situation.

I followed the hallway to the back, walking fast between the coin-activated videogames, the condom dispensers, the cigarette machines. I pushed out the back door and found myself on the sidewalk, facing the mortuary with its black and white picnic table and fake lawn.

A yellow cab was coming down the street. I couldn't believe it. There were no cabs in Cherokee Flats. Yet the car barreled towards me and screeched to a halt at my side, the back door open.

I heard confused sounds behind me. The bar's aluminum door with its flimsy screen was about to burst open.

I dove into the back seat without thinking, still holding the briefcase. The girl with green eyes was at the wheel. She turned around and asked me, "Where do you want to go today?"

It was a rhetorical question, because she already had her foot to the floor. The taxi fishtailed past the bar. I dug the detector from my pocket. It showed two signals, one steady, behind me, the other one pointing west, moving away fast.

"How far to Fayetteville?"

"Forty-five minutes."

I saw lights up ahead. Red flashers, a barrier.

"This state does have a seatbelt law," she said wryly, speeding up. "Just so you know."

Taking the hint, I quickly buckled up.

As we closed on the flashing lights, I made out several black shapes — men in uniform. The girl didn't slow down. She accelerated towards the barrier and, at the last moment, swerved aside, lifting the car on two wheels. We made an abrupt turn, even as I heard bullets whistling around us. Amazingly, she righted the taxi again, and soon we were speeding down a dirt road surround by fields. I couldn't stop a belated cry, more of fear than of pain, wondering if my vertebrae would never find their normal alignment again.

"Next time, bring your own car!" she said, laughing.

I started to doubt my own mental state. I had spent too much time inside the mine and too much time with Doctor Matt.

"You knew! You knew I'd be there!"

"You're complaining? "

"No…. That's not what I meant — "

"You were bound to end up here," she said, teasing me.

"One can't avoid one's destiny, I suppose," I intoned with some bitterness.

"You still have your detector?"

I looked at the instrument. The display still showed the two signals, one corresponding to the half of the artifact still in Cherokee Flats, the other headed for Fayetteville.

"They're taking samples to different labs," I said, then caught myself. How did she know about the detector? "Who exactly are you working for?"

"It's too late to tell you that," she said. "Or too early."

I ran my hand over my forehead, brought it back stained with dirt and blood. The girl handed me a first aid kit. "There's some water in the bottle."

She pointed at the landscape. Our tail was far behind us; we had left the mining area. I saw some farms, creeks, and little bridges that we passed at high speed.

176

"So, where do you want to go today?" she asked again.

"You sound like an ad for Microsoft," I said bitterly.

"Trust me, I'm not working for Microsoft." She laughed, a free, generous laugh that seemed to thaw something deep inside me. I had to work hard not to trust her.

"Of course not, since you're working for my partner, George Preston."

"You have a partner named George Preston?"

"Do you always answer questions with questions?"

"Ask me something I can answer."

I gave up, knowing I'd lost the game. The stationary signal behind us was fading fast; the moving one ahead of us started angling away from Fayetteville, going somewhere else.

"The airport!" I said.

"Twenty minutes," she answered curtly, taking the next exit. She didn't utter another word until she parked in front of the terminal. The sun was rising.

She reached back, hesitated, and touched my arm with unexpected tenderness. "Good luck," she said, and quickly turned away.

It was easy to spot the crewcut guy. He stood in line at the American Airlines counter, still wearing his leather jacket. His briefcase was attached to his wrist with a chain and a lock. I scanned the bank of departing flight monitors above him. My hunch was that someone working undercover for the so-called Mineral Services Company — hidden in a Navy base in the middle of Arkansas — would report to somebody in Washington, and this would likely take place in one of the myriad secret niches the military loved so much.

The fellow went through the scanner, triggering all sorts of bells and alarms. He pulled a card from his pocket and the security detail practically stood at attention. He proceeded without further challenge.

177

I ducked into a restroom to clean off the worst of the dirt and the blood, and when I judged myself as presentable as I was ever going to be, I joined the line snaking its way to American Airlines.

When I reached the ticket counter, I noted the attendant's name badge.

"Excuse me, Julia," I said. "I'm supposed to meet a colleague of mine. He may have passed through here already."

"Can you describe him to me?" she asked helpfully.

"Fairly tall. Crewcut. He's got a briefcase chained to his arm." I showed her my own briefcase.

"You must be doing important work," Julia said.

"I can't tell you what I do."

"I understand perfectly. Your colleague picked up his ticket five minutes ago. It's cleared to Washington and from there to Paris."

I managed to hide my surprise. So, Washington was just a stopover. The real secret was farther away. Much farther.

"Excellent. I'll join him on board."

I paid in cash, thanking Julia for her help.

"I'm happy to do whatever I can for my country, Sir."

Another night flight. Thankfully, Security had not asked me to explain the detector. It looked like an electronic organizer. The signal was very strong now; it pointed to seat 29A, where Crewcut, as I called him, seemed asleep. I would have liked to do the same, but images ran together in my mind: the death of Lewis, the green-eyed cabbie who turned into a stunt driver while deftly dodging my inquiries.

An earlier passenger had left a newspaper in the seat pocket. I tried to read, but the prose, and the news, simply discouraged me. I did notice an article in the regional section that mentioned the Corrals saucer landing. A private research group, CASUM, was suing another investigative outfit, ORPET, accusing it of plagiarism, libel and interference with a witness. Our experiment had launched a new cottage industry. Several books about Corrals were in the planning stages, as well as two television documentaries.

I still had the briefcase I'd recovered from the Blazer during the firefight with Colonel Lewis. Upon take-off I had stuffed it under the seat in front of me. I had a cup of black coffee and felt ready to study the contents.

Technical reports spilled from folders. They bore fancy scientific titles: "Asymmetrical Doppler Calibration tests on Sample B5," or "Reverse Engineering of Antigravitational Materials in a Crosby Space with Pulsed Negative Field."

In a side pocket I found a notebook filled with meeting schedules, telephone numbers and codes. The previous day someone had written in red ink, "Corrals – Type I event," and further down, "Intervention, 4 elements."

The latest handwritten entry read: "RV project, molecular substructure – Thalys – paradoxal signal – Bose-Einstein condensate."

None of that made any sense.

At Washington-Dulles airport, after a one-hour layover, we were ready to take off again for the flight over the Atlantic. I felt deeply troubled. My back still ached from the rough taxi ride. An inside voice told me that I was too old for such acrobatics. I wondered where Mark was, and whether I would ever see him again.

My heart felt heavy when I thought about Ricky.

Just before reaching Greenland, we were caught in an aurora borealis. Immense flags of intense color wrapped around us. They seemed to sweep against the plane, caressing it like a veil lifted by a breeze. The splendid sight reassured me. I managed to fall asleep.

18

Somewhere above Northern France my neighbor raised the window shade, waking me up. I had a headache and my ears were plugged. It took me a few minutes to verify that Crewcut was still in his seat. He was asleep.

What was I doing so far from home? From my normal activities? I had plunged into this adventure hoping to learn what was behind the phenomenon that had impacted my life so violently in Brazil, but at every turn I had encountered more and more questions, with a growing awareness of grand manipulations behind it all. Who was calling the shots from the shadows? Was there a point of control somewhere, or simply a chaos of opposing forces, constantly resetting their balance?

By the time the flight attendants served breakfast, I had sketched out a plan. The issue wasn't just to track the sample; I needed to find Mark. The police couldn't help me; this went too deep. So I was on my own. And I had come too far to return to California without some real answers. But what could I hope to accomplish by myself, in the middle of a mystery whose parameters went way over my head? I had some recollection of the Doppler Effect, but what did it mean for it to be asymmetrical? What was "a Crosby Space with Pulsed Negative Field?"

Shortly before landing, Crewcut got up to retrieve his briefcase from the top compartment. No doubt he wanted to make sure nobody had tampered with its valuable contents. He chained it again to his wrist. I sized him up. He didn't appear overly muscular, yet there was a balance to his movements, a cat-like grace that suggested martial arts training.

I followed his every step when we left the airplane. We went through customs at the same time. I took a taxi a few seconds after he climbed into a Mercedes that had been waiting for him at the curb. My driver, a Sikh with a large turban, managed to follow them as far as Le Bourget, but lost them by the time we reached the Périphérique Boulevard.

"What can I do, *Monsieur*? It's a Mercedes!" said the driver, as if that explained his blunder.

The detector showed a strong signal, but how would I ever track down the artifact in the anthills of Paris where Crewcut, no longer alone, could out-distance me without any difficulty? I thought back to the instructions on the papers I was carrying.

"Does the name Thalys mean anything to you?" I asked.

The Indian nodded. "Yes, Sir. It's a train, Thalys. The TGV for Belgium."

I decided on the spot. We rushed towards the *Gare du Nord*.

Like many Americans, I had always found Paris magical and incomprehensible, a combination of charming old objects and unique innovations. The city got on my nerves; it was exasperating; life in Paris required the mastery of numerous bizarre mechanisms, as absurd as the special pliers the French used when eating snails. I had made numerous business trips to Paris, never getting out to the countryside. I had a simplistic, linear view of Europe.

In the hall of the station, admiring the gray and burgundy locomotives with their magnificent curves, I was again struck by the aesthetic sense of the Old Continent. It made my purpose seem even more incongruous. If the Pentagon had a secret so fantastic it needed to bury it in the deepest levels of its bureaucracy — in such a strange way that even its own experts couldn't find trace of its budget — why hide it in Europe, which it distrusted so much?

Yet I had to follow my own logic. We had set a trap and the trap had worked. What Mark and I had seen in Cherokee Flats proved the existence of a project entrenched in the heart of the national security of the United States. The death of Colonel Lewis and the vast disinformation enterprise that surrounded the base where he died demonstrated the importance of the research, even today. Yet their technical team had not succeeded in discovering the nature of the phenomenon. Where would I get an answer to our questions?

Walking alongside the train, I saw Crewcut sitting in first class. I followed his example. He was alone, before a small table, reading a magazine by the light of a small lamp.

I checked the detector again: Crewcut still carried the artifact. Paris had only been a point of passage, not a relay for the team.

The train started with a soft acceleration. Lunch was proposed in four languages, with an efficiency that evoked the complexity of European institutions — an efficiency that American transportation had lost. My neighbor was a gray-haired gentleman whom I pictured as a member of such a grand multi-government organization. He was focusing on the day's newspapers. He went through the *Manchester Guardian*; next came *Le Monde Diplomatique*. We exchanged a few polite remarks.

An hour later, as he unfolded the *Corriere Della Serra* while the train dashed through a monotonous landscape, he called my attention to the fields and the woods where I saw only bucolic tranquility.

"We are going through the plain of Waterloo, Sir," he said. "We cross a border that no longer exists."

"Napoleon would be quite surprised," I answered. "It has taken quite a few battles to reach this result."

"The secret engine of history, Sir, is the tiredness of men."

182

That sentence was still in my mind when we reached the station in Brussels. Briefcase in hand, I followed Crewcut along the quay. Was he tired? What about those who employed him? How long would it take for the phenomenon to be acknowledged and the secret military data turned over to researchers? Was there any fundamental reason, any terrifying reality, that authorized a handful of men to keep this particular frontier sealed forever?

Nobody was waiting for Crewcut, and he didn't take a cab. He walked out of the station with his feline gait. I found it hard to keep up with him. He followed one avenue, crossed a square, and made a detour towards the center, according to an itinerary that he obviously knew very well. He was in a hurry. He never looked back.

We reached an austere area where dark buildings bore marble plates with gold lettering. He climbed a few steps and stopped before a double portal studded with heavy nailheads. He rang, said a few words in front of an invisible microphone. The door opened while I walked leisurely past — a carefree tourist — on the other side of the street.

I turned around and came back. The fine plaque read: "Banque Européenne de Placements Privés." Underneath, in smaller, discrete lettering: "Goldenstar Investment Funds."

Astounded by this discovery, I sought refuge in a nearby brasserie to weigh the consequences. If Goldenstar did represent one of the cogs in a very confidential research project, then a few elements of our adventure were cast in a different light. I had never heard of the B.E.P.P. It took two phone calls to American contacts to dredge up the information. It was the world's largest private bank, characterized by its immense discretion, only known through its subsidiaries like Goldenstar. Its headquarters were in Brussels, but it had notable branches in New York, London and Shanghai.

After a solid Belgian meal, I felt strong enough to go back to the place. It was my turn to climb the steps to the bank's forbidding door. I asked to see M. Joost van Vaart, giving my name through the intercom to the guard. Soon the door opened and I faced the financier. Standing six feet tall, he tilted his balding head to look down at me, a quizzical light in his eyes.

"Robert, so nice of you to pay us a visit!"

"What have you done with Mark Harris?" I asked without preamble.

"Don't worry! He is safe and sound. You will see him soon. May I suggest we begin with some mutual explanations? We have lost too much time."

He motioned to the guard, who pushed a button. As we waited together in the marble foyer, one detail caught my attention. Under an impeccable, well-tailored gray suit, Van Vaart wore a red wool pull-over adorned with chevrons. It gave him a bourgeois appearance, a hint of coquetry that clashed with his abrupt banking manners.

Crewcut appeared in the door frame, along with two men who each took me by an arm and marched me, police-like, to a scanner similar to those found at airport security checkpoints. They asked me, politely but firmly, to empty my pockets. They confiscated the detector and looked at it with interest. They went through the briefcase with intense scrutiny. Once they had ascertained that I wasn't armed and that I hadn't brought a bomb into the offices of the world's largest private bank, they returned me to van Vaart's authority and went away. With an urbane gesture, the Dutchman invited me to follow him to one of the salons inside the establishment.

I had tracked the signal all the way from Corrals, hoping that it would lead me to some secretive and formidable research center, an abode of high tech and space exploration. On the contrary, I found myself in an exquisite room paneled in rare woods and lined with bookcases filled with leather-bound tomes. Eight antique chairs surrounded a table covered with green felt that bore cut-crystal decanters. Above a marble fireplace hung a ravishing portrait: two ladies in long white dresses stood in a pastoral landscape, greyhounds at their feet. A page had gathered a bouquet of flowers and was handing it to them. When van Vaart saw my appreciation for the painting's charm, he offered a comment. "The sisters of the Baron de Charleroi, who founded this bank in 1857. In our professional activities, we seek to preserve certain fundamental values — starting with the sense of family, and the continuity of institutions."

"Is it the continuity of institutions that led you to become interested in unidentified phenomena? And to keep your investigations secret?"

If van Vaart detected the venom behind my words, he let it slide with elegance.

"Naturally," he said, offering me a seat in front of him. "Certain topics can exert social and psychological impacts out of proportion to their military or scientific importance."

"You don't consider the subject as scientifically important?"

"Others are handling that aspect of the problem."

"Your associates at the base of Cherokee Flats, perhaps?" I said. "Under cover of the Navy? People who don't hesitate to kill anyone who annoys them?"

If I had hoped for any expression of regret for the death of Lewis, I had come to the wrong place. Joost van Vaart simply shrugged, with a tired look towards the Baron's lovely sisters.

"Our American counterparts have some rough methods. You come from a violent society; I'm not teaching you anything new."

"Naturally, you disapprove of these methods."

"Come on, Robert," said van Vaart, showing indulgence to my anger. "I'm certain you know how a classified project has to be managed. The use of lethal force is an unpleasant aspect of that work."

"Obviously you're hiding something else. You know my partners, Mr. van Vaart. They may occasionally forgive me for being wrong, but never for being naive!"

"So you don't have a reputation for naiveté? Then you must have heard about Special Access Programs."

"I'm having trouble believing you manage a classified project like any other."

"We are not managing this project. We simply contribute a strategic component to it. Others are responsible for technical control."

"Lockheed? TRW? Northrop?"

"Keep going!" He didn't even try to hide his amusement. "You have left out Boeing, and a few others who are less visible in the media."

An assistant came in, carrying a tray with several glasses, mineral water, a coffee pot and cups that she silently put down on a credenza. As she left the room, two men entered. I recognized Belden and Demichel, who had taken part in our teleconferences. They acknowledged my presence without shaking hands.

"I believe introductions are unnecessary," said van Vaart. "I will only remind you that Dr. Belden, who manages our financial arbitrage services, holds a Ph.D. in theoretical physics from M.I.T., while Monsieur Demichel, who oversees our venture capital branch, is a skilled sociologist. Like yourself, he is a great lover of history. You ought to compare notes on the subject. He has authored a remarkable dissertation about non-conventional religions and sectarian phenomena."

"I'm sure that would be an interesting conversation," I said drily, "but that's not what brought me here."

"We know exactly what brought you here," broke in Belden just as drily. "It's this detector, and you are about to explain to us how it works."

He placed the confiscated device before me. John Brannan had designed and built that instrument. I might know how to use it, but I was incapable of explaining the stealth mode of the Nanotronics chips to a doctor in physics from M.I.T.

They tried everything, starting with flattery. They had taken apart our fake extraterrestrial evidence. They admired the circuits it contained. In Cherokee Flats, their technicians had reconstructed its function, but could not fathom how the signal could be detected hundreds of miles away without triggering their own sensors. They congratulated us on our technical prowess.

When they saw I wasn't biting, they started threatening me: sooner or later they would decipher our little secret. It would be a disaster for Nanotronics. They would sink our public offering on NASDAQ. My shares would have no value. I would be held responsible for our personnel being unemployed.

That left me unconcerned:

"That wouldn't be the first failure of a startup. Silicon Valley is rife with bankruptcies. Been there, done that, as they say."

"You haven't applied for a patent for this function of your circuits," pointed our Demichel. "We could do it ahead of you, and start a European company that would take over the market."

"That's your choice," I replied. "Don't forget that our laboratory notebooks would show anteriority on our side. You would run the risk of exposing your interest for unknown phenomena to the light of day. This wouldn't please your investors, or the wealthy people who entrust their savings to you."

Continuing in the same vein, I added, "Think about your sense of family, fundamental values.... There would be an international lawsuit. People would have to testify. You can't eliminate the whole planet."

That last remark hit a nerve.

"My dear Robert," said Dr. Belden, his voice as cool as the marble of the fireplace, "we are wasting time. Our assets amount to 60 billion dollars. With a 'B.' An sum equivalent to the foreign currency reserves of France. A lawsuit against Nanotronics does not scare us. Our attorneys will make sure many years pass before the Courts see the case. Would you care to remind me of how much cash you have?"

On this score I was beaten, and they knew it. That didn't give them the secret of the detector. They understood that their threats were as futile as the most syrupy protestations of admiration. Joost van Vaart rose.

"I suggest we stop at this point. You are our guest, naturally." He put a special emphasis on the word, "guest." "You will be taken to your apartments."

Crewcut reappeared. Belden and Demichel left the room without saying good-bye. I followed my guide, offering no resistance. He led me through a long hallway to an inner courtyard paved with large uneven stones that edged on a small park. To my left some old stables had been turned into garages for the senior bankers. To my right, a high, crenellated wall made it clear that I had lost access to the outside world. In front of me, framed by hundred-year-old trees, stood the admirable castle of the barons of Charleroi.

19

When I saw the castle, I stopped in my tracks. If I hadn't known the truth, the scene would have given me a feeling of peace. The stonework of the balconies, the twin guard towers with their machicolations, the sculptures that adorned the dormers, all that came from another age, preserved by a miracle. Did the miracle authorize the manipulation of strategic data of which heads of government were unaware?

Crewcut did not allow me the leisure to ponder the answer. He pushed me roughly towards the steps. I climbed the stairway to the manor. In the entrance hall with the white and black tiles we met one of his teammates, whom he introduced as Feldman. The fellow was tall and lean, about forty, balding, with a flat stomach, a scar on his forehead and an undulating gait that made it look like every muscle in his body was flowing, the gait of a Navy Seal.

Feldman took over. He led me to what he called my apartments — in other words, my prison cell — a fine room with thick stone walls, bars on the windows, a ravishing eighteenth century *secrétaire* that was worth a fortune, and two beds.

The bed on the left was occupied by Mark.

I shook him, without result. I yelled in his ear, "Mark! Mark Harris!" He finally opened his eyes, mumbled "Go to Hell!" and turned again towards the wall.

I went to bed without undressing. From time to time Mark said something aloud about stock market prices; he complained about some lights in his eyes that blinded him. Occasionally he called out to Ricky and started crying. It took me a long time to find the uneasy sleep of jet lag, which does nothing to release one's tiredness.

He must have been drugged, because my friend was still vaguely arguing aloud when I woke up.

Feldman came to fetch us. He brought us new clothes and toiletries. The bank, it seemed, expected me to show up fully dressed in a suit, like its own employees. I had a selection of ties. They even supplied me with new shoes to replace my sneakers, which had not survived the tribulations of Cherokee Flats and the fight among the gravel hills.

It was seven in the morning in Brussels. Mark treated me with an indifference that hurt my feelings. Several times I caught him giving me sidelong glances, as if he was trying to remember who I was. Joost van Vaart ushered us into a bland room devoid of decoration, where a breakfast was served in silence, after which we underwent another series of interrogations.

Later that day a dozen technicians from Cherokee Flats arrived and joined the Goldenstar team. They brought over the results of their own tests on our material. They were all anxious to understand how the detector worked. They had taken it apart during the night. Since neither Mark nor I were electronics experts, we spent some frustrating hours. They were sure our evasive answers demonstrated our bad faith, which was not entirely false in my case. As for Mark, he was still showing signs of genuine mental confusion.

They also demanded to know the slightest details of our Amazonian drama. They seemed to have bought into the fanciful theories of American ufologists who believed that the nature and strategy of extraterrestrials were hidden deep in the memory of witnesses. Feldman tried to hypnotize me

190

without much success, but they didn't try drugs on me, perhaps because that had failed with Mark. All they had gotten out of him was a tearful confession about his son.

Since that unhappy episode in Brazil, Mark had felt profoundly guilty. He blamed himself for the failure of his marriage and the death of Ricky, so that Goldenstar learned a lot of details about the private lives and intimate conflicts unfolding in the Harris couple's bedroom, and nothing at all about the phenomenon that had upset our lives.

Our captors must have realized they were taking the wrong tack, because in the evening they held a private consultation. They switched to a warm and friendly mode that I did not find any more genuine than their prior caustic attitude. Friends or foes, whether or not we cooperated with them, we were prisoners, and prisoners we were destined to stay. Colonel Lewis had stressed that the security of the project was obscene.

They brought us back to our room, going through another inside courtyard encased between high walls. Above the turrets and the watch towers, the Milky Way stretched across the sky in an arch. It seemed to say: "All this is mine, even the unavowable details of your petty human experience. Your weakness is my weakness. The secret you are seeking with such ineffectual eagerness is my own secret."

Should we take pity on the stars?

The following night, some movement next to my bed woke me up. Mark had gotten up, quite agitated. Taking a few angry steps to the window, he stared at the steel bars, and then came back towards me.

"I'm sorry, Robert! I don't know what kind of disgusting stuff they fed into me, but I barely recognized you yesterday."

"The main thing is that you snapped out of it. I really thought I'd lost you, when you stayed in the dunes like a fool and the helicopters picked you up."

191

"I couldn't imagine — " He gestured at the stylish furniture, barred windows, the walls outside. " — this whole story."

"Nobody could," I said. "Such a well-kept secret…lasting so long…without any answers. That's where the true secret lies! With their bankrupt imaginations, they're still searching for "extraterrestrials," unable to grasp another reality that's just as scientifically sound, but on the frontiers of modern knowledge."

"What difference does it make if it's 'extraterrestrial' or not?" agreed Mark. "It's a meaningless distinction, because those craft we saw were able to manipulate time and space. They can come out of anywhere, anytime. Even the Earth itself."

"In any case, Joost van Vaart's involvement in all this sheds some light on a few things — including the burglary at your house, and the crisis with Cheryl."

"What do you mean?"

"There's a detail that's been bothering me a long while: outside of you and me, only one person knew of Ricky's photographs. You told only one man. The burglary took place an hour later."

Sitting on the edge of the bed, Mark ran his fingers through his hair. "George Preston?"

"He's been very persistent about involving Goldenstar in our business."

Before we could discuss it further, Feldman came to pick us up. This time there was no ambiguity in our hosts' intentions.

"I have orders to take you to the bank offices," he said.

We crossed the courtyard and entered the modern building through a wide door and a marble hallway. In this section of the B.E.P.P, the paintings were bold abstract works. At major intersections stood plastic cubes on pedestals, lit up by invisible projectors. They contained bronze and copper sculptures, a commission of the bank to some contemporary artist.

Feldman pushed open a door. We were on an elevated platform overseeing a vast stockmarket room. A hundred traders in shirtsleeves sat before computer screens; assistants ran around in every direction. The three walls visible from our position were covered with figures, multicolored numbers that changed and constantly glided across. A special panel, high behind us, posted the value of the Nikkei index.

"Our stock market activities represent about five percent of the volume of Nasdaq and as much on Euronext, in an average day. New York is still asleep. The team you see here is specialized in Asian assets."

We followed Feldman along a balcony where three large flat screens displayed CNN, BBC and a Chinese information channel. The sound was off. We could see an American politician giving a speech, but the only noise was that of the hundred computer keyboards in the room.

At the end of the balcony, another door led to a suite of wide offices in a quieter setting, almost an academic atmosphere. A gold plaque read,

"WORLDWIDE RISK ANALYSIS BRANCH."

I began to understand. As I stared at the words, it dawned on me that if the world's largest private bank sheltered a center specializing in world-scale risk analysis, then the phenomenon we had experienced must be a factor in all its calculations. It would be involved, if only as a wild card, a joker, a low-probability event whose potential impact was huge.

"We are going to explain to you what our role is," said van Vaart when he greeted us in a conference room where coffee and croissants were waiting for us. A giant map took an entire wall.

Dr. Belden, very courteous, poured me a glass of orange juice. He wore beige trousers, a yellow shirt and a tie with tiny red squares. He had left his jacket in another office.

Van Vaart was dressed in a dark suit and a sky blue pull over, pleasantly enlivened by stripes of a darker hue. I pictured his wife knitting by the fireplace. This notion amused me, of Mrs. van Vaart clicking away with her needles at home while her husband analyzed planetary risks.

"The project has evolved over time," began the Dutchman. "The Americans have picked up some physical traces. As you have guessed, what the media tells the public is pure and simple disinformation. The amateur organizations are used to amplify fake rumors."

"Wait a minute!" interrupted Mark. "There's also some serious literature: Keyhoe, Ruppelt, Hynek, the Lorenzens.... They've shown that a significant proportion of the cases correspond to real phenomena. The Blue Book project, for example. You can look at those files on the Internet now, and it's full of stuff that ought to be of interest to scientists."

"But no proof," Belden said dryly. "That lies elsewhere."

"Precisely," echoed van Vaart. "The evidence is somewhere else. Blue Book reported to the public relations flacks inside the Pentagon, not to the operational offices."

He gave a sign. A projector came to life at the far end of the room while a screen unrolled itself silently along the wall. A list of entries appeared.

"Here is a summary of the chronology. The very first classified project concerning UFOs in the United States was launched in 1943, at the Bureau of Standards. The goal was to identify the foo-fighters, the luminous objects that followed Allied bombers — "

"As well as German planes," interjected Demichel with a smile, "which we only realized after the war when the Nazi archives were analyzed."

Van Vaart had mentioned that his younger associate was a passionate historian. He must have been happy in this project.

"We reach the date of June 24, 1947, with the sighting by pilot Kenneth Arnold, which captivates the media and makes popular the expression "flying saucers." This leads the Pentagon to set up a classified project called "Sign" on January 22, 1948, with Professor Hynek as the scientific adviser. One out of five cases remains unexplained, even after study by technical experts."

"You can well imagine the frustration of U.S. strategic analysts," commented Belden. "These objects are playing with their fighters and their radars. What will the taxpayers say? And what about Congress, which controls the budget?"

"That, in turn, led to Project Grudge on December 16, 1948, and eventually Blue Book, which would last from 1951 to January 1969. It was terminated when the University of Colorado decreed that the subject had no scientific value — "

"Despite the fact that one out of three cases defied explanation by their committee — an even greater mystery than in the days of Sign!" said Demichel with glee. He added, "Science is a wonderful thing, so malleable! You can bend it to say whatever you want!"

"We already know all that," I pointed out impatiently. "I've seen much the same chronology in several books."

"You may not know what happened behind the curtain. In 1952 alone there were over 1,500 reports of unidentified objects sent to Air Force centers. Communications were saturated. Nobody at the Pentagon was laughing anymore. The so-called rationalist scientists who'd 'explained' the phenomena were discredited. It was their turn to feel silly!"

"Think of it in terms of risk analysis," went on Demichel. "An astute enemy could have triggered a false saucer wave, blocking military communications and saturating the public with stories about Martians while their strategic bombers attacked America with impunity! That led to yet another series of secret meetings."

"We reach a turning point now," said van Vaart. "On July 28, 1952, U.S. Air Force Intelligence is fed up with the uncertainty surrounding the sightings. It decides that the phenomenon must be regarded as a serious problem, to be studied intensely by technical means. Efforts will be made to obtain tangible, physical data, ignoring reports from the public that are judged as too unreliable and tenuous. Project Blue Book will continue, but only as an adjunct, a mailbox to give ordinary citizens a place to send their sightings. The military will concentrate the efforts of its experts on instrumented observations made with radar, cameras or other tracking systems, and physical samples. This leads to a critical point, the gathering of scientific heavyweights on January 13, 1953, under the chairmanship of Professor Robertson, a physicist with a worldwide reputation. They get together at the request of the Air Force "

"And the CIA," added Demichel.

"And the Battelle Memorial Institute," said Belden. "Don't forget that Battelle had just completed the first statistical study on unexplained cases. The project head, a Dr. Cross, sends a letter, classified SECRET, to the CIA to ask "what could and could not be discussed" with the scientists. In this document, which has become known as the "Pentacle Memorandum," he proposes to launch more specialized studies. He also suggests that the meeting be postponed or disbanded."

"Again, I've seen this stuff in the literature," I pointed out. "What does it have to do with your activities?"

"The Robertson committee represents a major bifurcation in the study of the phenomenon," said Belden.

"The modern history of the research," continued Van Vaart, "starts with that 1953 meeting. Contrary to what Battelle proposed, the committee did meet. It recommended a campaign of disinformation to actually discourage ordinary citizens from reporting UFOs."

"Such reports had become useless, since the Pentagon was now focused on instrumented reports," added Demichel.

"They also decided to plant informants in the groups of ufology amateurs, to collect information and discourage any civilian research that would interfere with the secret projects. These informants – or their successors -- are still in place."

"What's the point?" asked Mark.

"They wanted to leverage the popular belief in extraterrestrials as a weapon of psychological warfare. For example, when a military prototype or a secret missile crashed somewhere, the public was fed the rumor that the object was a flying saucer. They are used to discredit anyone who comes a bit too close to the real stuff."

I recalled the words of Stephanie Sheldon at the Senate restaurant, recounting the Bennewitz story: "You are on dangerous ground." I thought of Doctor Matt, the dottering old drunkard, drinking bourbon as he waited for the Devil to come and pick him up.

If Satan did exist — and took an interest in those who'd betrayed mankind on this topic — he would enjoy a wide selection of guilty targets.

"The Soviets were never fooled by any of that, by the way," the Dutchman went on. "They understood what was going on and learned quickly. They used the same trick to hide their intercontinental rockets from the world when they violated international treaties about strategic satellites."

"It's a game everybody can play," summarized Belden, rubbing his hands together as if he had just heard an excellent joke. "And the funny thing is, it still goes on today: the newspapers talk about a wave of UFOs over India to hide the massive use of stealthy American drones over Kashmir and Pakistan, tracking Al Kaida. Every time, the ufology groups see an opportunity to get recognition and exposure in the media, so they jump on the rumor and amplify it."

"And that is how science has been fooled!" concluded van Vaart. "A conference of civilian experts, gathered at the United Nations in New York in 1978 under the presidency of General Secretary Kurt Waldheim, stipulated that major nations should exchange their data on the subject. There was a formal recommendation to the political committee of the UN. It was shot down by the U.S. and Great Britain, who argued that it would cost too much! In the meantime, another project, far more serious, followed its course in total secrecy. First harbored under the purview of the Pentagon, it was later transferred to private industry to help preserve confidentiality. Corporations like ours are not subject to the laws regarding the freedom of information and public disclosure."

Mark raised his hand. "This is where I don't follow you anymore. I can understand why aerospace firms might have an interest in secretly studying the sighting data. But where do you come in? You have no special knowledge in reverse engineering, as far as I can see."

"It seems you have misunderstood the nature of our work, Mr. Harris," the Dutchman said calmly. "We have an investment capability that dwarfs the resources of all aerospace companies combined. When a government — any government — wants to launch a satellite, manufacture new rockets or design a new bomber, it has to find the cash somewhere. We have both the cash and the know-how to manage complex projects."

"There are others with similar capabilities," insisted Mark.

"That may be so, but perhaps they are less flexible. Or less discreet. Remember, we are a private bank; few people even know our name."

Demichel gestured towards the map of the world that stretched over the back wall. "We are experts in analysis and risk management. We have at our disposal, in every country, professional networks of representatives and men who can serve as liaison with officials at high government levels. They are more reliable and less visible than CIA agents — especially given the current political disarray in Washington, where intelligence analysts don't even know where to report from one day to the next! A particular government does not necessarily need, or want, American involvement, but sooner or later it needs hard cash. Is that a true statement, Mr. Harris?"

Mark did not react. He seemed stunned by the turn of events.

"We are objective in a cynical way," added Belden. "Our function in the grand scheme of the world economy is not to posture as moralists or tort redressers. We are free of political allegiance. If the planet warms up, we leave it to others to cool it down again. Instead, we ask where agriculture is likely to disappear and if the permafrost will, some day soon, turn into wheat fields. We will sell our assets in Kansas and finance harvesters to be sold in the Yukon. If there is an increase in heroin sales in London, we ask who makes the needles."

Demichel got up, stretched his long arms and commented, "If it is true that unknown objects fly over the Amazon basin, that piece of data could impact our long-term models of the planetary economy. It introduces an uncertainty factor, which we must measure. This is not a question of believing or disbelieving, you understand. We are not ideologues. We only strive to arrive at a reliable estimation of a statistical risk."

"And that is why you are about to lead us to the very place where this happened to you," concluded van Vaart as he turned off the projector.

A weak sun was occasionally visible through heavy clouds in a gray sky, a typical sky of Belgian paintings with its unique, subtle light. The clouds looked like flying mountains, incongruous Himalayas pushed away from the coast by the North Sea wind. Joost van Vaart got up without giving us a chance to react to his statement and calmly informed us that lunch would be served in the next room.

20

Joost van Vaart impatiently followed the movements of a heavy-set Dutch woman who wore a uniform with the colors of the bank. She cleared the table after our lunch. She piled up the plates on a rolling table and pushed it into the hallway. She returned with cups and a coffee pot.

"I cannot see any reason to hide anything from you at this point of our project," stated the financier once she had gone back to the kitchen.

I had expected this moment. We were indeed part of the project now. Nobody had hinted at this — hinting wasn't the style of the house — and we had not been asked to sign a statement of non-disclosure; but it was obvious that we knew too much for Goldenstar to ever release us.

"Tomorrow evening we fly to Rio, where we catch another plane to Belèm. My colleagues and I have concluded that you will be all the more useful to us if you have a good picture of the whole situation."

I glanced at Mark. He had remained very calm, emptying his coffee cup while listening to van Vaart with intense attention. He set down his cup and laid both hands flat on the table. Demichel seemed bored, his eyes scanning the paintings around the dining room walls: country scenes under dark skies, hints of light oozing out of menacing clouds. Though not an expert in art, I would have sworn that one — familiar to me from art books — was a Bruegel original. As for Dr. Belden, he was staring at the bottom of his cup as if reading the future in coffee stains.

What would Dr. Matt have said, if he had witnessed the scene? He had joined the project as a young medical technician, recruited to help scientists who studied the effects of radiation on humans and the design of future space capsules. He had lost his way and his mind in the complexities of a network of secrets so bizarre that nobody believed his story. Now Joost was dangling before us the hope of knowing the whole truth. I should have been tingling with anticipation; the mystery was nearing its end. Matt would have seen this as a descent to Hell, but the *Banque Européenne de Placements Privés* did not harbor this kind of mystical torment.

"We have custody of an object that will interest you," said van Vaart. "As I have told you, the Americans are in charge of physical tests. We are aware of your...escapade...in Cherokee Flats. No need to play at charades; the analysis has made no headway. We know nothing more today than we did when we captured the object."

Demichel seemed to wake up from his rèverie. He raised his hand as if to grasp an invisible string and said in a conciliatory tone, "It's not entirely correct to say we know nothing more. In reality, we've discovered everything the object is NOT. It does not have a well-defined surface; it does not contain a fixed light source, although it is luminous; it does not occupy a precise volume; it does not seem to have an inside and an outside, if you see what I mean."

I did not.

"It is only detectable as a membrane that changes shape in an arbitrary manner; it is harder than carbon steel but eminently flexible; it induces dangerous physiological effects, speeding up aging in humans. Imagine the problems we've had recruiting and keeping technicians to help us, as well as security teams."

"And how did you gain 'custody' of this object?" asked Mark.

The question had been on my lips for a while. I noted the way Mark had phrased it. It was a true banking expression, this idea of "taking custody." From what van Vaart and Demichel had just said, I rather had the feeling the thing did not belong to anybody.

"Everybody associates the phenomenon with the Air Force, because so many observations come from pilots or radar operators. However, just in the Blue Book files, you would find hundreds of cases from the Navy."

Mark and I exchanged glances. The base in Cherokee Flats was guarded by Navy personnel.

"Go back to 1953," said Belden, taking over the story in a voice as warm and informal as van Vaart's was dry and stern. "We are in a period of the Cold War when Battelle's projects are in full expansion. The Pentacle Memorandum is penned by Cross and his team of metallurgical experts. They are secretly working on titanium aluminate, a critical alloy for high performance jets. In the meantime, the Blue Book project continues to accumulate observations from the public, and sometimes from military personnel. The Pentagon looks at all this indifferently, counting on Professor Hynek to explain the phenomena. The decisions of the Air Force regarding cases with physical evidence are followed to the letter in total secrecy. And in November 1953 everything changes: a British submarine detects a whole series of underwater objects drifting in the vicinity of Fanning Island, in the Pacific."

"I've never heard of Fanning Island," said Mark.

"It's a circular island, an atoll about 15 miles wide, an old crater with a magnificent lagoon, coral and coconut palms. It's also one of the first relays of the trans-Pacific cable, selected because of its ideal position a few degrees from the Equator."

"Today, Fanning, along with Christmas Island and the Gilbert Islands, belongs to the Republic of Kiribati," added Belden.

"While keeping an eye on the integrity of the cable, a submarine of Her Gracious Majesty's Navy discovered several submerged objects. When the captain realized the objects were fragments of a craft destroyed by some sort of catastrophic failure, he passed the news up his chain of command, and of course they told the Americans about it. Surface ships were dispatched from Pearl Harbor, with cranes and grappling tools. Two objects were fished out. One was sent to the Cherokee Flats laboratory. The other one remained with the British services, who eventually deposited it with us."

"I assume that isn't the kind of deposit that arrives every day in your coffers," said Mark, as amused as I was by the choice of words.

"Indeed," continued Belden, allowing himself a thin smile, "but we often take as security automobiles, valuable objects, or scientific equipment, like any bank. Sometimes we have to seize aircraft, boats. Even yachts! You wouldn't believe how destitute their owners turn out to be when we ask them to pay what they owe us!"

"We have occasionally had to care for a space satellite," added van Vaart. "When the British sent us their fragment, we built a special laboratory, a clean room."

"And nobody got wind of it?" Mark asked, surprised.

"That was six years after Kenneth Arnold's sighting had launched the flying saucer myth. Journalists only got excited about cases in the air, which the public knew through some popular books. The fantasies of the Contactees like George Adamski, who spoke of flying around the solar system with his Venusian friends, were all over the world press, with the encouragement of American services who were exploiting the story. Against such a backdrop, our secrets were well-kept. Later, in the 1980s, the project ran the risk of being outed. That's when we

203

dredged up the fake Roswell crash stories again, complete with the tale of the Alien Autopsy. Every TV producer in the world fell willingly into that trap."

"Works every time," said Belden, laughing. "You are the first researchers to come up with a scheme — what you call your 'stratagem' — to figure out what was really going on. You may be the first who truly wanted to find out."

Van Vaart got up. "We will show you the object we study. Do not expect to witness phenomena like those you experienced in Brazil. We think what we have is a section detached from a much larger craft. The one in Arkansas looks like an airplane wing. Ours is more like the hull of a ship."

We followed van Vaart along a hallway that led to an observation room. It opened onto a cleanroom laboratory as large as the trading floor we had visited earlier. In the center rested the object detected by the Royal Navy in the depths of the Pacific.

It was a "thing," rather than an object.

Objects do not change shape every second, going from an inert, quasi-metallic phase to a phosphorescent irradiation, pulsating like the skin of a medusa. Solid objects do not go through other solid objects. That is one of the so-called "laws" of physics. Objects have well-defined surfaces.

Demichel had warned us: the thing did not follow any of these rules. It appeared to play with our space. Sometimes it was transparent and so faintly lit that it seemed about to vanish. The next instant, it emerged like an aircraft carrier steaming out of a fog bank, massive with its armor, bristling with masts, turrets and antennas.

We saw a series of lightning strikes. In spite of the distance, we felt peculiar effects. They began with a syncopated melody, and the perception of strong smells, sulfur the main component. As in Cherokee Flats, I was seized by a migraine, the pain localized at the base of the brain. I felt carried away into a world of colors and music where I lost my bearings. A blinding light swept through my impressions, saturating what was left of my terrestrial existence.

I found the garden again, the flowers with the shimmering wings. I saw the woman who had smiled so tenderly. She invited me to follow her along a walkway that led to a hill. Curiously, night had fallen by the time we reached the top; she disappeared. I was left alone, facing the stars that whirled around my vision.

Colorful images, as vibrant as the stained glass panels of a cathedral, glided from one side of the horizon to the other. They displayed complex scenes where color planes fused together, then separated again. I felt someone was trying to teach me a lesson, but the scene became blurred when swirls of fog rolled across the field, palpitating like the heart of a small bird.

I opened my eyes. The light went back to its normal hue, gradually. The room enclosed us again in its blandness. I became aware of Mark and Demichel, who had grabbed me by the arms to prevent me from falling. I leaned on the window ledge in time to see the thing lose its luminosity, returning to its original dimensions and shape. As van Vaart had told us, it looked like the hull of a ship, resting bottom up.

"We think it's some sort of a hologram," whispered Demichel.

"A hologram with mass," added Belden. "We have turned this problem over to optical experts. Everything works as if the object was emitting frozen light."

"As you are no doubt aware, there is no such thing as a hologram with mass," corrected Demichel with a guffaw. "Or frozen light, for that matter. So there you are."

Very pale, Mark simply acquiesced with a blink. I knew I should ask some questions, but my brain simply couldn't formulate them. Whatever the thing was, it certainly did not qualify as a UFO: it was not an object and it came out of the water. Unidentified it certainly remained.

"Can we stop at this point, for today?" begged Mark, running his hand over his forehead and then wiping the sweat with his handkerchief.

"Of course," answered van Vaart. "The first few times, it's very draining."

He pushed a button; a metal curtain came down over the window.

"Now it should be clear to you why your experience is of interest to us," the Dutchman went on, as our little group walked back to the room where we had had lunch. "After all these years, we only have an extremely limited understanding of the phenomenon. The team in Cherokee Flats suffers from low morale. Modern physics gives us some tools to describe the effects, but no theoretical structure to understand the cause."

Feldman was waiting for us in the Bruegel room. He had spread a series of nautical charts over the large table. They showed the entire delta of the Amazon, on a scale where we could see the smallest anchorage. Maximum and minimum depths were labeled in feet. He also had aerial navigation charts displaying the runways, radio beacons and radar stations of the *Primero Comar*, the first air zone of Brazil, together with the patterns for the international airports at Manaus and Belèm, and the communication frequencies for pilots.

"We're going to put you to work," said van Vaart, his index finger pointing to the harbor in Belèm. "We have hired a ship that is on its way to the place where you had your experience. It carries all necessary instrumentation to conduct soundings of the river, detect any submarine structure, analyze the nature of any underwater technology, human or not."

"And what's our role in all this?" asked Mark.

"You will help us retrace your exact route. I've already told you: we fly tomorrow."

"What if we don't agree with the plan?"

"Dear Mr. Harris, it is not for the pleasure of conversation that we have just briefed you on our projects. You yourself noted that the security around the work was "obscene." Let us not allow obscenities to affect the nature of our relationship."

"Furthermore," said Demichel, "a few weeks in Brazil, all expenses paid, aboard a first-class ship, how can you turn that down!"

21

The *Charleroi* left the harbor in Belèm early in the afternoon in muggy weather, as gray and heavy as the steel gates that closed the hangar behind us. To keep the expedition secure, Crewcut and Feldman had decided not to hire any Brazilian sailors, who glared at us as we took the channel with deliberate slowness. Their banter and occasional jeering accompanied our departure.

We sailed with a 15-man crew, most of them from the American project. Others had been hand-picked from the Goldenstar technical staff. They were no more accustomed than we to navigating below the Equator. They sweated profusely while dropping the lines and maneuvering the yacht.

"They could have picked something a bit more discreet," said Mark as we admired the lines of the ship, which was blinding white, its three bridges equipped with antennas and spotlights, security systems and radar.

The ship's control room stood much higher than the trawlers and cargo ships in the harbor. Along the piers, dockworkers sprawled in the shadow of mountains of boxes and containers, waiting for the afternoon heat to pass. Anybody in his right mind in Belèm was taking a siesta. Only foreigners like us, moved by an arrogance underlined by the incongruous majesty of this billionaire's vessel — pride of the Antwerp naval works — would navigate among fishermen's barks, crazy enough to sail up the big river. The daily thunderstorm had yet to come, so in addition to the oppressive physical discomfort I'd had since morning, I now felt depressed as well. We had stumbled on a key, or at least a piece of the answer about the secret project, but we did not know anything more about the phenomenon. Everything we had learned about the course of the research led to a discouraging assessment of the limitations of men's science and — even more to the point — their meanness. On the other hand, I detected a new sense of exaltation within Mark. This surprised me. He couldn't stand still; he would lean over the railing to study the river, to extract its secrets, as if he were about to discover some cosmic truth, or a reason to go on living.

The faraway shore was only a dark band receding to the horizon when the storm finally came. It began with a rolling series of lightning strikes, accompanied by thunderous drumming as if an invisible fist was hammering the first three blows before a theater play. The first act began immediately: the clouds burst all together, pouring cataracts over the boat, drowning the shore, reducing our visibility to a few yards.

Feldman went up to take the wheel, shifting to radar navigation. Mark remained with me in the shelter of a gangway, where we could see the river without being drenched. The wind came, lifting waves so high they shook the boat and made it drift further out.

While he made sure nothing was loose on deck and that the *Charleroi* was ready to face the storm, Crewcut kept a weary eye on us. We were sailing towards Colares when a new series of waves and violent bursts of wind made us drift to the North. Despite the crew's efforts, mountains of water caught us across the way, pushing the ship like a toy. A trawler or a simple sailboat would not have survived these blows. An hour later the rain was still falling heavily. The waves seemed to merge into a massive current, an irresistible flux that made a mockery of our engines, rudders and radars. The idea that we should stop to sound the river, which had seemed interesting during our conversations in the sumptuous salons of Goldenstar, had become ridiculous amidst the magnificent chaos of all the elements unleashed around us.

The current was dragging the ship, along with the rush of flotsam carried by the river: trees branches and giant algae, live crocodiles, fragments of buildings swept off some construction site, bodies of animals drowned upstream. A blast of wind pushed the vessel on one side, throwing us against the cabin wall. When the *Charleroi* straightened herself out, precariously balanced on top of a fluid mountain, she had lost her engines.

Crewcut and his men got busy with pumps and emergency systems. Mark and I went down to help them. Several partitions had burst under the shock and doors were unhinged. As we ran along a gangway, passing a holding space, Mark suddenly halted, fascinated by what he saw inside. Up ahead the crew was yelling in fear, close to panic, concerned with cracks and fuel leaks. Mark had taken a step inside the warehouse. He was inspecting a row of crates. He pointed at the labels. The crates contained underwater mines. Deeper within, tied to steel beams, an exploration robot equipped with torpedoes and several heavy-duty salvage instruments demonstrated the real goal of our expedition: the crew wasn't content to simply observe the phenomenon and detect its origin, they intended to attack it.

The *Charleroi* was a warship.

Disgusted by what we'd just seen, we went up to the top deck, determined to find a way to escape from the Goldenstar crew before they could use us as bait in their senseless project.

I'll never know for sure what wrecked the *Charleroi*. Perhaps a mass of vegetation sweeping past us had tangled the twin propellers. Or perhaps the violent waves shoving us side to side had flooded the engines. In any case, the yacht became just another piece of rubbish dragged along by the current. And then the cataracts from the sky seemed to merge with the relentless rush of the angry river to throw the *Charleroi* against the rocky shore of an islet.

Caught between a cliff and the surf-beaten shoals, the ship was still in one piece; but there was a tear in the hull, as told by the clamors of the crew, and it was only a matter of time before the yacht would break into fragments that the pitiless river would carry away.

"Here's our chance!" yelled Mark, pointing at the *Charleroi's* emergency lifeboats. Though shaken by repeated blows and drenched by the waves, we had remained on the relatively sheltered side during the storm. Finding the strength to unhook and inflate one of the rafts, we threw it overboard. As we did, Feldman spotted us. He charged forward, tackled Mark and yelled for me to stop. I was already sliding off the smooth rear deck of the ship, unable to stop my course even if I had wanted to. Once in the water, rid of my cane and my shoes, I caught up with the raft and steered it away, thankful to the shipbuilders of Antwerp for their foresight in designing such a wonderful device.

I gave up trying to start the engine: the current had taken hold of the raft, lifting it like a cork far from the wreckage of the *Charleroi*, and I whirled around in eddies, grabbing hold of ropes to keep from falling out, as the storm took me where it would.

There was no navigation system on board, only a compass that showed that I was drifting North and an emergency radio beacon I did not turn on. Another hour and the flow became calmer. Now the rain was steady, a tepid shower replacing the blasts of rain that had fallen in bucketfuls.

The sky was still gray but the heat had abated during the storm, so that I was able to rest at last, sitting at the bottom of the raft where I found drinkable water and food rations in a watertight compartment.

As the river slowed, so did the passage of time. Overwhelmed by recent events — by nature itself — I felt

211

myself surrendering to an incomprehensible fate. Debris kept me company: trees torn from the soil, rotten boards, a fragment of fabric that looked like a sail.

A sail? I took an oar and paddled towards it to pick it up, lift it out of the river. It bore an insignia I recognized. It was a torn fragment of the boat we had once sailed, Mark and I. With Ricky.

The river was quiet now, as majestic in its calm as it had been hideously savage a few hours before. The horizon was a dark line between the silver spread of the water and the mountains of dark, receding clouds. On my knees in the raft — the better to hold onto the fabric — I pulled on the white sail, its frayed edges reminding me of the tearing of my own life, the tragedy of Mark and his son. If only I could find my bearings and manage to survive, I swore I would bring back this piece of our boat in memory of our ordeal.

As I was about to start the engine and trigger the distress signal, a disturbance in the water caught my attention. Beyond the folds of the sunken sail, a black object had surfaced. It came out of the water very fast, took on human form, and stretched itself upon the surface to float before me. A hand reached up to sweep off a diving mask, and I found myself looking at a familiar face. It was the girl with the green eyes.

"There's no escaping you, is there?" I shouted, still kneeling in my rubber raft.

I felt anger, yet I had hoped to see her again.

"There is no escaping one's destiny," she said with a wry smile. "Didn't you tell me that one evening, back in Arkansas?"

It seemed both very strange and very simple that here, in the middle of the Amazon, we should be resuming the conversation we began in a taxicab racing away from the mines of Cherokee Flats!

Ours was a story begun at the edge of Banderas Bay: at Mary's Café, she had helped us escape from would-be killers; in Cherokee Flats, she had arrived in the nick of time to save my life. She had made it possible for me to renew the chase, to implement the stratagem, to discover the heart of the secret project.

Mark and I had created a game, never realizing that we were mere pawns on somebody else's board.

"Your superiors must be very pleased!" I shouted derisively. "You appeared at every turn, every critical point." I wanted to hurt her.

"They were looking for the same thing you were," she said with that easy laugh of hers, teasing me with her provocative eyes. "Perhaps it was you guiding me, have you thought of that? You led me to Goldenstar. I was just following you."

She now stood on a glistening platform. Tossing her mask into the river, she unzipped and stepped from her diving suit. She wore a white one-piece uniform that was skintight. Daughter of the hurricane or priestess of the river, she seemed at ease in every role.

"What are you looking for, once and for all?" I cried in despair. "What's the secret?"

"You can reveal a secret only to someone who has already guessed it," she answered, freeing her long hair. It danced about her, driven by some mysterious wind.

"Then I suppose I'm a prisoner once again," I said in disgust. "Or are you going to throw me back into the water, too insignificant to be kept in your nets?"

"Don't worry," she said coldly. "I never take prisoners."

Her face seemed to glow. Her eyes became translucent emeralds. I realized a light was rising behind me, illuminating her, projecting my shadow on the river. Just as I turned, I saw a flash, felt a sudden headache. My forehead was damp with perspiration.

Lights danced on the river. They spun and whirled like fireflies, then gathered together to form solid objects. I turned in circles, confused, until I realized my mistake.

A gigantic craft was silently coming out of the water. As it did so, I felt all my questions being answered. It wasn't a spaceship. It wasn't even a ship, or a technology. It didn't look like an airplane wing, like the one in Cherokee Flats, or a boat hull, like the one in Brussels. It was a world. I gaped at multicolored landscapes, superstructures that lit up the overcast, glittering arches like stained-glass windows. A huge cathedral was merging with Brazil, bringing with it new sounds, unknown materials, entire continents. It lifted the flow of the river, dropping it again in enormous cascades.

I turned back to the girl. She was still smiling.

"Don't go on looking for the vessels of your technological phantasms," she said. "Instead, look for other worlds, ones under your very noses. You wanted extraterrestrials? You could find your true human nature, and your own cosmic destiny in the bargain."

"Cosmic or not, terrestrial or not, you've made some mistakes!" I said spitefully.

"When we make mistakes, we try to correct them," she answered.

She pointed beyond me, and I turned to see a silhouette forming there, emerging from the folds of the mirage — or from a universe parallel to ours?

"Robert!" cried a child as he ran towards me. "Where's Dad?"

Magistrates of destiny, judges of the infinite, how should we call those who come from the edge of time, to remind us of the order of the worlds? We had computed galaxies and drawn up repertories of pulsars. Good students, we had made catalogues of all the forms of life we decreed possible, light-year by light-year, until our relativity was exhausted with the supply of dark matter. What had we forgotten? Which parameter had we left out of the equation?

A portal had opened up in the confusion of my own consciousness, a portal of forgetfulness and delight about the intelligences from beyond, which does not close even at death. Too briefly, I was a guest of the extravagant beings who go through our daily realities at will, marking us with their paradoxical signs. Those non-reproducible phenomena, the scorn of savants, we call anomalies: do they bear the imprint of forces that are not human, yet close to us?

Back at Goldenstar, experts speculated that the object in their clean room must be a hologram, some manipulation of light from an unknown source. A thousand groups of amateur ufologists, meanwhile, bent the worldwide web under the weight of speculation about extraterrestrials, inspired by 1950 science fiction augmented by Star Wars. They were all wrong.

French poet Paul Eluard had written that he believed in other worlds to the extent that were "inside this one." How should we classify their inhabitants, like the girl with green eyes standing in front of me? Extraterrestrials, if you wish, unless we dare to acknowledge that the Terrestrial also has access to other dimensions?

Those portals of infinity, once triggered in my mind, remained wide open, even when I found myself floating aboard the raft with Ricky. While the other universe receded into the evening haze, I knew, with succulent knowledge, what I had gained.

The lights disappeared and the girl vanished with them.

"It was like a dream," said Ricky. "I thought I saw inside the world."

I showed him how to turn on the distress beacon. Meanwhile, as we drifted westward, I tried to guess at our position. An hour later we still hadn't seen the shore, but a fat helicopter of the *Força Aérea* weighed down on us to fish us out. Night was falling when they dropped us off at the base at *Primero Comar*, behind barbed wire.

22

We were spending our last hours in the facilities that controlled the airspace over the Amazon delta — an area equivalent to the size of Texas. The military had intervened to rescue the shipwrecked crew of the *Charleroi*. Half a dozen men had died in the storm, including Felman and Crewcut, but Mark Harris had survived. I saw him come out of the last helicopter, supported by young bearded soldiers who seemed amused by their adventure.

Pausing on the tarmac, his exhaustion evident, he slowly surveyed the crowd. His eyes lit up when he spotted me. Then, catching sight of Ricky, he burst into tears.

Under guard, we were taken to a series of tents set up in an empty field behind the hangars. It was hot in there, and mosquitoes bothered us all night; but that was nothing compared to the roar of the jets testing their engines on secondary runways nearby.

The following days were spent answering endless questions that demonstrated how deeply the Brazilian services understood the phenomenon. An Air Force intelligence colonel, in particular, seemed to have devoted special interest to the problem. He was a heavy-set man, always strapped in a uniform of perfect cleanliness. He summoned us into his vast office where fans stirred warm humid air, loaded with the stale smell of his cigars.

It did not take long for the colonel to sort through the crew members of the *Charleroi*. He put the simple sailors on the earliest flights back to Europe. One of Feldman's henchmen had a rough time with the interrogators. He was sent off to jail, pending more information requested from Brussels.

The colonel spent a lot of time with us. He interrogated us separately, in perfect English, then compared my answers with those of Mark. Each time, a secretary transcribed our testimony.

In spite of Mark's protests, Ricky had to submit to the same questions, alone with the officers. They did not appear surprised when Ricky spoke about his excursion aboard the strange craft.

After a few days spent debriefing us, the colonel summoned the inhabitants of the villages we had visited. Manuel, who had steered our sailboat, was grilled for six hours by a brutish lieutenant in a cell from which the poor man thought he would never come out alive.

We saw terrified fishermen come and go, and even the girl who ran the bodega where Ricky and his father had bought mineral water was brought in. Some of the local witnesses did not speak Portuguese, but the colonel and his men were fluent in the dialects of the Amazon.

Later I learned that the colonel was half Indian — through his mother — and quite familiar with the traditions of the tribes that lived along the river.

The following week the *Primero Comar* received orders that changed the colonel's behavior towards us. His officers moved us out of the tents where we had been temporarily sheltered, and put us up in new buildings next to their headquarters; but it was clear that they didn't want to hear another word from us about unknown objects. In Brasilia the government was under political pressure. New presidential elections were looming, and the Air Force had better things to do than fishing out Americans who were busy chasing extraterrestrials.

They placed before us a document certifying that we would never mention our adventures to the media. We signed it without hesitation.

217

"Some interesting things are happening in the United States," said Mark Harris the next morning as we were having breakfast. At the *Primero Comar*, that was the best meal of the day, in part because the sun did not yet give off its full power, and because Brazilian coffee smelled so good.

Mark kept an arm around Ricky, who watched young aviators playing soccer in the dust. He held a copy of the previous day's *New York Times* that he'd picked up at the officer's mess. On page 11 a paragraph noted that the U.S. Navy had decided to close off several bases, including a training center, curiously located in Arkansas, whose existence no one had suspected before. In the finance pages we read that several aerospace firms had warned analysts about a likely drop — abrupt, unscheduled and unexplained — in their R&D budget for the following quarters.

The science section devoted much space to a just-published report by Professor Randolph concerning the phenomena observed in Corrals. Already a best-seller, the document had received the official stamp of the Academy of Sciences. It contained some "especially novel" reflections relative to the psycho-sociology of rural environments. It left no doubt about the nature of the phenomenon: a combination of the rising moon and re-entry of an old Russian rocket. The disorientation of the witnesses, due to stress, had done the rest and started the outrageous rumors.

Professor Randolph's insightfulness amounted to a theoretical breakthrough, gushed the *New York Times* review. The stress of the rural *milieu* had been widely underestimated, until now, by academic researchers. Known as "the Randolph Effect," this observation would surely inspire many a dissertation in sociology.

"In other words, Corrals is another urban legend," I said with amusement.

"Except that it happens in the countryside," answered my friend.

218

"Those are the worst kind!"

We burst out laughing. It was good to re-embrace our old camaraderie, laughing at each other's weak jokes.

The following afternoon we were told to gather our things for departure. I had adjusted to camp life, enjoying my time with Ricky and Mark; several young airmen had gotten in the habit of bringing gadgets for the boy, and had become our friends.

About 5 P.M. a lieutenant drove up in a Jeep. He brought a flight plan and warm respects from the colonel, along with trinkets from local artisans, as gifts, "for your families, in memory of Amazonia."

"You really don't want to come with us?" Mark asked me.

On the other side of the runway, a big aircraft was being rolled out of the hangars, specially fuelled for a flight to California. The Brazilians were wasting no time. They wanted us gone before any journalists or nosy foreign "diplomats" became aware of our existence.

"I think I'll spend a little more time around here," I answered. "The colonel has agreed to let me stay in a hotel in town, to get to know the country better. As long as I'm not under his responsibility any more, and I keep my mouth shut...."

"I was hoping you'd come back to California," Mark said with sadness. "You're gonna miss Silicon Valley."

"Nanotronics can work without me."

He followed my eyes to the harbor and the river, towards the islands of Colares and Mosqueiro where my life had twice been shaken. He understood from the look on my face.

"You're thinking about her, admit it," he said.

I said only, "Her, and others like her."

"Why did they help us?"

"They shared our agenda — to flush out the classified project that studied the phenomenon. We were following our artifact. They followed us. They had to neutralize the black project. They hold the only true secret."

"Your story isn't over...."

I walked with them to the edge of the runway. With tears in my eyes, I embraced Ricky.

Things would be simpler in the future. Nothing was left of the Pentagon's scheme. As for the Goldenstar group, it was good enough at computing financial risk to understand the situation: there was no upside to asking too many questions about the strange meteorological phenomenon that had triggered a storm and smashed the *Charleroi*.

The field of new opportunities is vast indeed, when you manage sixty billion dollars. The loss of one ship and a few staff members is a page that is easy to turn.

I had no concerns regarding the initial public offering of Nanotronics, or the future of Joost van Vaart, who got along so well with George Preston.

The afternoon storm had not yet burst when I embarked on the little sailboat I had bought from a fisherman in Belèm. At the end of the channel I heard the plane that was taking Ricky and Mark to San Francisco. I looked up in time to see the big Hercules, painted in camouflage, flying over the roofs of the city, subjecting all to the roar of its huge propellers. Silently, I wished good luck to my friend. In the same vein, I said goodbye to my past life.

The current grew very strong as the boat emerged from the harbor, so I didn't bother raising the sail. Soon the shore was far behind. Halfway to Colares the sky became fringed with golden shimmerings. Circular lights appeared under the surface. In the translucent humidity of the Amazon, another world was lifting up. It rose to meet me, emerging from the other dimensions of time. It fused slowly, gently, with the Earth.

THE END

CPSIA information can be obtained
at www.ICGtesting.com
Printed in the USA
LVHW091653220419
615083LV00006B/39/P